P9-DEK-991

ALCATRAZ

★VERSUS★ THE EVIL LIBRARIANS

BY BRANDON SANDERSON

Scholastic Press ★ New York

YA
SAN

Library of Congress Cataloging-in-Publication Data

Sanderson, Brandon.
   Alcatraz Smedry versus the evil Librarians / by Brandon Sanderson.
      p.   cm.
   Summary: On his thirteenth birthday, foster child Alcatraz Smedry receives a bag of sand which is immediately stolen by the evil Librarians who are trying to take over the world, and Alcatraz is introduced to his grandfather and his own special talent, and told that he must use it to save civilization.
   ISBN-10: 0-439-92550-9 (hardcover)
   ISBN-13: 978-0-439-92550-1
   [1. Fantasy.   2. Librarians—Fiction.   3. Grandfathers—Fiction.   4. Clumsiness—Fiction. 5. Humorous stories.]   I. Title.

PZ7.S19797A1c 2007
[Fic]—dc22
2006038378

12 11 10 9 8 7 6 5 4 3 2 1   7 8 9 10 11 12/0

Printed in the U.S.A.   23
First printing, October 2007

Book design by Alison Klapthor

For my father, Winn Sanderson, who bought me books

AUTHOR'S FOREWORD

I AM NOT A GOOD PERSON.

OH, I KNOW WHAT THE STORIES SAY ABOUT ME. THEY CALL ME OCULATOR DRAMATUS, HERO, SAVIOR OF THE TWELVE KINGDOMS. . . . THOSE, HOWEVER, ARE JUST RUMORS. SOME ARE EXAGGERATIONS; MANY ARE OUTRIGHT LIES. THE TRUTH IS FAR LESS IMPRESSIVE.

WHEN MR. BAGSWORTH FIRST CAME TO ME, SUGGESTING THAT I WRITE MY AUTOBIOGRAPHY, I WAS HESITANT. HOWEVER, I SOON REALIZED THAT THIS WAS THE PERFECT OPPORTUNITY TO EXPLAIN MYSELF TO THE PUBLIC.

AS I UNDERSTAND IT, THIS BOOK WILL BE PUBLISHED SIMULTANEOUSLY IN THE FREE KINGDOMS AND INNER LIBRARIA. THIS PRESENTS SOMETHING OF A PROBLEM FOR ME, SINCE I WILL HAVE TO MAKE THE STORY UNDERSTANDABLE TO PEOPLE FROM BOTH AREAS. THOSE IN THE FREE KINGDOMS MIGHT BE UNFAMILIAR WITH THINGS LIKE BAZOOKAS, BRIEFCASES, AND GUNS. HOWEVER, THOSE IN LIBRARIA — OR THE HUSHLANDS, AS THEY ARE OFTEN CALLED — WILL LIKELY BE UNFAMILIAR WITH THINGS LIKE OCULATORS, CRYSTIN, AND THE DEPTH OF THE LIBRARIAN CONSPIRACY.

TO THOSE OF YOU IN THE FREE KINGDOMS, I SUGGEST THAT YOU FIND A REFERENCE BOOK — THERE ARE MANY THAT WOULD DO — TO EXPLAIN UNFAMILIAR TERMS TO YOU. AFTER ALL, THIS BOOK WILL BE PUBLISHED AS A BIOGRAPHY IN YOUR LANDS, AND SO IT IS NOT MY PURPOSE TO TEACH YOU ABOUT THE STRANGE MACHINES AND ARCHAIC

WEAPONRY OF LIBRARIA. MY PURPOSE IS TO SHOW YOU THE TRUTH ABOUT ME, AND TO PROVE THAT I AM NOT THE HERO THAT EVERYONE SAYS I AM.

IN THE HUSHLANDS — THOSE LIBRARIAN-CONTROLLED NATIONS SUCH AS THE UNITED STATES, CANADA, AND ENGLAND — THIS BOOK WILL BE PUBLISHED AS A WORK OF FANTASY. DO NOT BE FOOLED! THIS IS NO WORK OF FICTION, NOR IS MY NAME REALLY BRANDON SANDERSON. BOTH ARE GUISES TO HIDE THE BOOK FROM LIBRARIAN AGENTS. UNFORTUNATELY, EVEN WITH THESE PRECAUTIONS, I SUSPECT THAT THE LIBRARIANS WILL DISCOVER THE BOOK AND BAN IT. IN THAT CASE, OUR FREE KINGDOM AGENTS WILL HAVE TO SNEAK INTO LIBRARIES AND BOOKSTORES TO PUT IT ON SHELVES. COUNT YOURSELF LUCKY IF YOU'VE FOUND ONE OF THESE SECRET COPIES.

FOR YOU HUSHLANDERS, I KNOW THE EVENTS OF MY LIFE MAY SEEM WONDROUS AND MYSTERIOUS. I WILL DO MY BEST TO EXPLAIN THEM, BUT PLEASE REMEMBER THAT MY PURPOSE IS NOT TO ENTERTAIN YOU. MY PURPOSE IS TO OPEN YOUR EYES TO THE TRUTH.

I KNOW THAT IN WRITING THIS I SHALL MAKE FEW FRIENDS IN EITHER WORLD. PEOPLE ARE NEVER PLEASED WHEN YOU REVEAL THAT THEIR BELIEFS ARE WRONG.

BUT THAT IS WHAT I MUST DO. THIS IS MY STORY — THE STORY OF A SELFISH, CONTEMPTIBLE FOOL.

THE STORY OF A COWARD.

CHAPTER 1

So, there I was, tied to an altar made from outdated encyclopedias, about to get sacrificed to the dark powers by a cult of evil Librarians.

As you might imagine, that sort of situation can be quite disturbing. It does funny things to the brain to be in such danger — in fact, it often makes a person pause and reflect upon his life. If you've never faced such a situation, then you'll simply have to take my word. If, on the other hand, you *have* faced such a situation, then you are probably dead and aren't likely to be reading this.

In my case, the moment of impending death made me think about my parents. It was an odd thought, since I hadn't grown up with them. In fact, up until my thirteenth birthday, I really only knew one thing about my parents: that they had a twisted sense of humor.

Why do I say this? Well, you see, my parents named me

Al. In most cases, this would be short for Albert, which is a fine name. In fact, you have probably known an Albert or two in your lifetime, and chances are that they were decent fellows. If they weren't, then it certainly wasn't the name's fault.

My name isn't Albert.

Al also could be short for Alexander. I wouldn't have minded this either, since Alexander is a great name. It sounds kind of regal.

My name isn't Alexander.

I'm certain that you can think of other names Al might be short for. Alfonso has a pleasant ring to it. Alan would also be acceptable, as would have been Alfred — though I really don't have an inclination toward butlery.

My name is not Alfonso, Alan, or Alfred. Nor is it Alejandro, Alton, Aldris, or Alonzo.

My name is Alcatraz. Alcatraz Smedry. Now, some of you Free Kingdomers might be impressed by my name. That's wonderful for you, but I grew up in the Hushlands — in the United States itself. I didn't know about Oculators or the like, though I did know about prisons.

And that was why I figured that my parents *must* have had a twisted sense of humor. Why else would they name their child after the most infamous prison in U.S. history?

On my thirteenth birthday, I received a second confirmation that my parents were indeed cruel people. That was the day when I unexpectedly received in the mail the only inheritance they left me.

It was a bag of sand.

I stood at the door, looking down at the package in my hands, frowning as the postman drove away. The package looked old — its string ties were frayed, and its brown paper packaging was worn and faded. Inside the package, I found a box containing a simple note.

Alcatraz,

Happy thirteenth birthday!
Here is your inheritance, as promised.
Love, Mom and Dad

Underneath the note, I found the bag of sand. It was small, perhaps the size of a fist, and was filled with ordinary brown beach sand.

Now, my first inclination was to think that the package was a joke. You probably would have thought the same. One thing, however, made me pause. I set the box down, then smoothed out its wrinkled packaging paper.

One edge of the paper was covered with wild scribbles —
a little like those made by a person trying to get the ink in a
pen to flow. On the front there was writing. It looked old
and faded — almost illegible in places — and yet it accurately spelled out my address. An address I'd been living at
for only eight months.

Impossible, I thought.

Then I went inside my house and set the kitchen
on fire.

Now, I warned you that I wasn't a good person. Those
who knew me when I was young would never have believed
that one day *I* would be known as a hero. *Heroic* just didn't
apply to me. Nor did people use words like *nice* or even
friendly to describe me. They might have used the word
clever, though I suspect that *devious* may have been more
correct. *Destructive* was another common one that I heard,
but I didn't care for it. (It wasn't actually all that accurate.)

No, people never said good things about me. Good people don't burn down kitchens.

Still holding the strange package, I wandered toward my
foster parents' kitchen, lost in thought. It was a very nice
kitchen, modern looking with white wallpaper and lots
of shiny chrome appliances. Anyone entering it would

immediately notice that this was the kitchen of a person who took pride in their cooking skills.

I set my package on the table, then moved over to the kitchen stove. If you're a Hushlander, you would have thought I looked like a fairly normal American boy, dressed in loose jeans and a T-shirt. I've been told I was a handsome kid — some even said that I had an "innocent face." I was not too tall, had dark brown hair, and was skilled at breaking things.

Quite skilled.

When I was very young, other kids called me a klutz. I was always breaking things — plates, cameras, chickens. It seemed inevitable that whatever I picked up, I would end up dropping, cracking, or otherwise mixing up. Not exactly the most inspiring talent a young man ever had, I know. However, I generally tried to do my best despite it.

Just like I did this day. Still thinking about the strange package, I filled a pot with water. Next I got out a few packs of instant ramen noodles. I set them down, looking at the stove. It was a fancy gas one with real flames. My foster mother Joan wouldn't settle for electric.

Sometimes it was daunting, knowing how easily I could break things. This one simple curse seemed to dominate my entire life. Perhaps I shouldn't have tried to fix dinner. Perhaps I should simply have retreated to my room. But what was I to do? Stay there all the time? Never go out because I was worried about the things I *might* break? Of course not.

I reached out and turned on the gas burner.

And, of course, the flames *immediately* flared up around the sides of the pan, far higher than should have been possible. I quickly tried to turn down the flames, but the knob broke off in my hand. I tried to grab the pot and take it off of the stove. But, of course, the handle broke off. I stared at the broken handle for a moment, then looked up at the flames. They flickered, catching the drapes on fire. The fire gleefully began to devour the cloth.

Well, so much for that, I thought with a sigh, tossing the broken handle over my shoulder. I left the fire burning — once again, I feel I must remind you that I'm not a very nice person — and picked up my strange package as I walked out into the den.

There, I pulled out the brown wrapper, flattening it against the table with one hand and looking at the stamps. One had a picture of a woman wearing flight goggles, with an old-fashioned airplane in the background behind her. All of the stamps looked old — perhaps as old as I was. I turned on the computer and checked a database of stamp issue dates and found that I was right. They had been printed thirteen years ago.

Someone had taken quite a bit of effort to make it *seem* like my present had been packaged, addressed, and stamped over a decade earlier. That, however, was ridiculous. How would the sender have known where I'd be living? During the last thirteen years, I'd gone through dozens of sets of foster parents. Besides, my experience has been that the number of stamps it takes to send a package increases without warning or pattern. (The postage people are, I'm convinced, quite sadistic in that regard.) There was no way someone could have known, thirteen years ago, how much postage it would cost to send a package in my day.

I shook my head, standing up and tossing the M key from the computer keyboard into the trash. I'd stopped trying to stick the keys back on — they always fell off again anyway. I got the fire extinguisher from the hall closet, then walked back into the kitchen, which was now quite thoroughly billowing with smoke. I put the box and extinguisher on the table, then picked up a broom, holding my breath as I calmly knocked the tattered remnants of the drapes into the sink. I turned on the water, then finally used the extinguisher to blast the burning wallpaper and cabinets, also putting out the stove.

The smoke alarm didn't go off, of course. You see, I'd broken *that* previously. All I'd needed to do was rest my hand against its case for a second, and it had fallen apart.

I didn't open a window but did have the presence of mind to get a pair of pliers and twist the stove's gas valve off. Then I glanced at the curtains, a smoldering ashen lump in the sink.

Well, that's it, I thought, a bit frustrated. *Joan and Roy will never continue to put up with me after this.*

Perhaps you think I should have felt ashamed. But what was I supposed to do? Like I said — I couldn't just hide in my room all the time. Was I to avoid living just because life was a little different for me than it was for regular people? No. I had learned to deal with my strange curse. I figured that others would simply have to do so as well.

I heard a car in the driveway. Finally realizing that the kitchen was still rank with smoke, I opened the window and began using a towel to fan it out. My foster mother — Joan — rushed into the kitchen a moment later. She stood, horrified, looking at the fire damage.

I tossed aside the towel and left without a word, going up to my room.

★

"That boy is a disaster!"

Joan's voice drifted up through the open window into my room. My foster parents were in the study down on the first floor, their favorite place for "quiet" conferences about me. Fortunately, one of the first things that I'd broken in the house had been the study's window rollers, locking the windows permanently open so that I could listen in.

"Now, Joan," said a consoling voice. It belonged to Roy, my foster father.

"I can't take it!" Joan sputtered. "He destroys everything he touches!"

There was that word again. *Destroy.* I felt my hair bristle in annoyance. *I don't destroy things,* I thought. *I break them. They're still there when I'm finished, they just don't work right anymore.*

"He means well," Roy said. "He's a kindhearted boy."

"First the washing machine," Joan ranted. "Then the lawn mower. Then the upstairs bath. Now the kitchen. All in less than a year!"

"He's had a hard life," Roy said. "He just tries too hard — how would you feel, being passed from family to family, never having a home . . . ?"

"Well, can you blame people for getting rid of him?" Joan said. "I —"

She was interrupted by a knock on the front door. There was a moment of silence, and I imagined what was going on between my foster parents. Joan was probably giving Roy "the look." Usually, it was the husband who gave "the look," insisting that I be sent away. Roy had always been the soft one here, however. I heard his footsteps as he went to answer the door.

"Come in," Roy said, his voice faint, since he now stood in the entryway. I remained lying on my bed. It was still early evening — the sun hadn't even set yet.

"Mrs. Sheldon," a new voice said from below, acknowledging Joan. "I came as soon as I heard about the accident." It was a woman's voice, familiar to me. Businesslike, curt, and more than a little condescending. I figured those were all good reasons why Ms. Fletcher wasn't married.

"Ms. Fletcher," Joan said, faltering now that the time had come. They usually did. "I'm . . . sorry to —"

"No," Ms. Fletcher said. "You did well to last this long. I can arrange for the boy to be taken tomorrow."

I closed my eyes, sighing quietly. Joan and Roy had lasted quite long — longer, certainly, than any of my other recent sets of foster parents. Eight months was a valiant effort when taking care of *me* was concerned. I felt a little twist in my stomach.

"Where is he now?" Ms. Fletcher asked.

"He's upstairs."

I waited quietly. Ms. Fletcher knocked but didn't wait for my reply before pushing open the door.

"Ms. Fletcher," I said. "You look lovely."

It was a stretch. Ms. Fletcher — my personal case-worker — *might* have been a pretty woman, had she not been wearing a pair of hideous horn-rimmed glasses. She perpetually kept her hair up in a bun that was only slightly less tight than the dissatisfied line of her lips. She wore a simple white blouse and a black ankle-length skirt. For her, it was a daring outfit — the shoes, after all, were maroon.

"The kitchen, Alcatraz?" Ms. Fletcher asked. "Why the kitchen?"

"It was an accident," I mumbled. "I was trying to do something nice for my foster parents."

"You decided that you would be kind to Joan Sheldon — one of the city's finest and most well-renowned chefs — by burning down her kitchen?"

I shrugged. "Just wanted to fix dinner. I figured even *I* couldn't mess up ramen noodles."

Ms. Fletcher snorted. Finally, she walked into the room, shaking her head as she strolled past my dresser. She poked my inheritance package with her index finger, harrumphing quietly as she eyed the crumpled paper and worn strings. Ms. Fletcher had a thing about messiness. Finally, she turned back to me. "We're running out of families, Smedry. The other couples are hearing rumors. Soon there won't be any place left to send you."

I remained quiet, still lying down.

Ms. Fletcher sighed, folding her arms and tapping her index finger against one arm. "You realize, of course, that you are worthless."

Here we go, I thought, feeling sick. This was my least favorite part of the process. I stared up at my ceiling.

"You are fatherless and motherless," Ms. Fletcher said, "a parasite upon the system. You are a child who has been given a second, third, and now *twenty-seventh* chance.

And how have you received this generosity? With indifference, disrespect, and *destructiveness!*"

"I don't destroy," I said quietly. "I break. There's a difference."

Ms. Fletcher sniffed in disgust. She left me then, walking out and pulling the door closed with a snap. I heard her say good-bye to the Sheldons, promising them that her assistant would arrive in the morning to deal with me.

It's too bad, I thought with a sigh. *Roy and Joan really are good people. They would have made great parents.*

CHAPTER 2

Now, you're probably wondering about the beginning of the previous chapter, with its reference to evil Librarians, altars made from encyclopedias, and its general feeling of "Oh, no! Alcatraz is going to be sacrificed!"

Before we get to this, let me explain something about myself. I've been many things in my life. Student. Spy. Sacrifice. Potted plant. However, at this point, I'm something completely different from all of those — something more frightening than any of them.

I'm a writer.

You may have noticed that I began my story with a quick, snappy scene of danger and tension — but then quickly moved on to a more boring discussion of my childhood. Well, that's because I wanted to prove something to you: that *I am not a nice person.*

Would a nice person begin with such an exciting scene,

then make you wait almost the entire book to read about it? Would a nice person write a book that exposes the true nature of the world to all of you ignorant Hushlanders, thereby forcing your lives into chaos? Would a nice person write a book that proves that Alcatraz Smedry, the Free Kingdoms' greatest hero, was just a mean-spirited adolescent?

Of course not.

I awoke grumpily that next morning, annoyed by the sound of someone banging on my downstairs door. I climbed out of bed, then threw on a bathrobe. Though the clock read 10:00 A.M., I was still tired. I had stayed up late, lost in thought. Then Joan and Roy had tried to say good-bye. I hadn't opened my door to them. Better to get things over without all that gushing.

No, I was not happy to be reawoken at 10:00 A.M. — or, actually, *any* A.M. I yawned, walking downstairs and pulling open the door, prepared to meet whichever assistant Ms. Fletcher had sent to retrieve me. "Hell —" I said. (I hadn't intended to swear, but a boisterous voice cut me off before I could get to the "o.")

"Alcatraz, my boy!" the man at the doorway exclaimed. "Happy Birthday!"

"— o," I said.

"You shouldn't swear, my boy!" the man said, pushing his way into the house. He was an older man who was dressed in a sharp black tuxedo and wore a strange pair of red-tinted glasses. He was quite bald save for a small bit of white hair running around the back of his head, and this puffed out in an unkempt fashion. He wore a similarly bushy white mustache, and he smiled quite broadly as he turned to me, his face wrinkled but his eyes alight with excitement.

"Well, my boy," he said, "how does it feel to be thirteen?"

"The same as it did yesterday," I said, yawning. "When it was *actually* my birthday. Ms. Fletcher must have told you the wrong date. I'm not packed yet — you're going to have to wait."

I tiredly began to walk toward the stairs.

"Wait," the old man said. "Your birthday was . . . yesterday?"

I nodded. I'd never met the man before, but Ms. Fletcher had several assistants. I didn't know them all.

"Rumbling Rawns!" the man exclaimed. "I'm late!"

"No," I said, climbing the stairs. "Actually, you're early. As I said, you'll need to wait."

The old man rushed up the stairs behind me.

I turned, frowning. "You can wait downstairs."

"Quickly, boy!" the old man said. "I can't wait. Soon you'll be getting a package in the mail, and —"

"Stop. You know about the package?"

"Of course I do, of course I do. Don't tell me it already came?"

I nodded.

"Blistering Brooks!" the old man exclaimed. "Where, lad? Where is it?"

I frowned. "Did Ms. Fletcher send it?"

"Ms. Fletcher? Never heard of her. Your parents sent that box, my boy!"

He's never heard of her? I thought, realizing that I'd never verified the man's identity. *Great. I've let a lunatic into the house.*

"Oh, blast!" the old man said, reaching into his suit pocket and pulling out a pair of yellow-tinted glasses. He quickly exchanged the light red ones for these, then looked around. "There!" he said, rushing up the stairs, pushing past me.

"Hey!" I called, but he didn't stop. I muttered quietly to myself, following. The old man was surprisingly spry for his age, and he reached the door to my room in just a few heartbeats.

"Is this your room, my boy?" the old man asked. "Lots of footprints leading here. What happened to the doorknob?"

"It fell off. My first night in the house."

"How odd," the old man said, pushing the door open. "Now, where's that box . . . ?"

"Look," I said, pausing in the doorway. "You have to leave. If you don't, I'm going to call the police."

"The police? Why would you do that?"

"Because you're in my house," I said. "Well . . . my ex-house, at least."

"But you let me in, lad," the old man pointed out.

I paused. "Well, now I'm telling you to leave."

"But why? Don't you recognize me, my boy?"

I raised an eyebrow.

"I'm your grandfather, lad! Grandpa Smedry! Leavenworth Smedry, Oculator Dramatus. Don't tell me you don't remember me — I was there when you were born!"

I blinked. Then frowned. Then cocked my head to the side. "You were there . . . ?"

"Yes, yes," the old man said. "Thirteen years ago! You haven't seen me since, of course."

"And I'm supposed to remember you?" I said.

"Well, certainly! We have excellent memories, we Smedrys. Now, about that box . . ."

Grandfather? The man had to be lying, of course. *I don't even have parents. Why would I have a grandfather?*

Now, looking back, I realize that this was a silly thought. Everybody has a grandfather — two of them, actually. Just because you haven't seen them doesn't mean they don't exist. In that way, grandfathers are kind of like kangaroos.

At any rate, I most certainly *should* have called the police on this elderly intruder. He has been the main source of all my problems ever since. Unfortunately, I didn't throw him out. Instead, I just watched him put away his yellow-tinted spectacles, retrieving the reddish-tinted ones again. Then he finally spotted the box on my dresser, scribbled-on brown paper still sitting beside it. The old man rushed over eagerly.

Did he send it? I wondered.

He reached into the box, taking out the note with an oddly reverent touch. He read it, smiling fondly, then looked up at me.

"So, where is it?" Grandpa Smedry — or whoever he really was — asked.

"Where is what?"

"The inheritance, lad!"

"In the box," I said, pointing at the package.

"There isn't anything in here but the note."

"What?" I said, walking over. Indeed, the box was empty. The bag of sand was gone.

"What did you do with it?" I asked.

"With what?"

"The bag of sand," I said.

The old man breathed out in awe. "So, it really came?" he whispered, eyes wide. "There was actually a bag of sand in this box?"

I nodded slowly.

"What color was the sand, lad?"

"Um . . . sandy?"

"Galloping Gemmells!" he exclaimed. "I'm too late! They must have gotten here before me. Quickly, lad. Who's been in this room since you received the box?"

"Nobody," I said. By this point, as you can imagine, I was growing a little frustrated and increasingly confused. Not to mention hungry and still a bit tired. And a little sore from gym class the previous week — but that isn't exactly all that relevant, is it?

"Nobody?" the old man repeated. "Nobody else has been in this room?"

"Nobody," I snapped. "Nobody at all." Except ... I frowned. "Except Ms. Fletcher."

"Who *is* this Ms. Fletcher you keep mentioning, lad?"

I shrugged. "My caseworker."

"What does she look like?"

"Glasses," I said. "Snobbish face. Usually has her hair in a bun."

"The glasses," Grandpa Smedry said slowly. "Did they have ... horn rims?"

"Usually."

"Hyperventilating Hobbs!" he exclaimed. "A Librarian! Quickly, lad, we have to go! Get dressed; I'll go steal some food from your foster parents!"

"Wait!" I said, but the old man had already scrambled from the room, moving with a sudden urgency.

I stood, dumbfounded.

Ms. Fletcher? I thought. *Take the inheritance? That's stupid. Why would she want a silly bag of sand?* I shook my head, uncertain what to make of all this. Finally, I just walked over to my dresser. Getting dressed, at least, seemed like a good idea. I threw on a pair of jeans, a T-shirt, and my favorite green jacket.

As I finished, Grandpa Smedry rushed back into my bedroom, carrying two of Roy's extra briefcases. I noticed a leaf of lettuce sticking halfway out of one, while the other seemed to be leaking a bit of ketchup.

"Here!" Grandpa Smedry said, handing me the lettuce briefcase. "I packed us lunches. No telling how long it will be before we can stop for food!"

I raised the briefcase, frowning. "You packed lunches inside of briefcases?"

"They'll look less suspicious that way. We have to fit in! Now, let's get moving. The Librarians could already be working on that sand."

"So?" I said.

"So!" the old man exclaimed. "Lad, with those sands, the Librarians could destroy kingdoms, overthrow cultures, dominate the world! We need to get them back. We'll have to strike quickly, and possibly at great peril to our lives. But that's the Smedry way!"

I lowered the briefcase. "If you say so."

"Before we leave, I need to know what our resources are. What's your Talent, lad?"

I frowned. "Talent?"

"Yes," Grandpa Smedry said. "Every Smedry has a Talent. What is yours?"

"Uh . . . playing the oboe?"

"This is no time for jokes, lad!" Grandpa Smedry said. "This is serious! If we don't get that sand back . . ."

"Well," I said, sighing. "I'm pretty good at breaking things."

Grandpa Smedry froze.

Maybe I shouldn't play with the old man, I thought, feeling guilty. *He may be a loon, but that's no reason to make fun of him.*

"Breaking things?" Grandpa Smedry said, sounding awed. "So it's true. Why, such a Talent hasn't been seen in centuries. . . ."

"Look," I said, raising my hands. "I was just joking around. I didn't mean —"

"I knew it!" Grandpa Smedry said eagerly. "Yes, yes, this improves our chances! Come, lad, we have to get moving." He turned and left the room again, carrying his briefcase and rushing eagerly down the stairs.

"Wait!" I cried, chasing after the old man. However, when I reached the doorway, I paused.

There was a car parked on the curb outside. An old car. Now, when you read the words *old car*, you likely think of a beat-up or rusted vehicle that barely runs. A car that is old, kind of in the same way that cassette tapes are old.

This was not such a car. It was not old like cassette tapes are old — it wasn't even old like records are old. No, this car was old like Beethoven is old. Or, at least, so it seemed. To me — and, likely, to most of you living in the Hushlands — the car looked like an antique. Kind of like a Model-T.

But that was just my assumption.

The point is that many times, the first thing a person presumes about something — or someone — is inaccurate. Or, at the very least, incomplete. Take the young Alcatraz Smedry, for instance. After reading my story up to this point, you have probably made some assumptions. Perhaps you're — despite my best efforts — feeling a bit of sympathy for me. After all, orphans usually make very sympathetic heroes.

Perhaps you think that my habit of using sarcasm is simply a method of hiding my insecurity. Perhaps you've decided that I wasn't a cruel boy, just a very confused one. Perhaps you've decided, despite my feigned indifference, I didn't *like* breaking things.

Obviously, you are a person of very poor judgment. I would ask you to kindly refrain from drawing conclusions that I don't explicitly tell you to make. That's a very bad habit, and it makes authors grumpy.

I was none of those things. I was simply a mean boy who didn't really care whether or not he burned down kitchens. And that mean boy was the one who stood on the doorstep, watching Grandpa Smedry waving eagerly for him to follow.

Now, *perhaps* I'll admit that I felt just a little bit of longing. A . . . wishfulness, you might say. Getting a package that claimed to be from my parents had made me remember days long ago — before I realized how foolish I was being — when I had yearned to know my real parents. Days when I had longed to find someone who *had* to love me, if only because they were related to me.

Fortunately, I had outgrown those feelings. My moment of weakness passed quickly, and I slammed the door closed and locked the old man outside. Then I went to the kitchen to get some breakfast.

That, however, is when someone drew a gun on me.

CHAPTER 3

I'd like to take this opportunity to point out something important. Should a strange old man of questionable sanity show up at your door — suggesting that he is your grandfather and that you should accompany him upon some quest of mystical import — you should flatly refuse him.

Don't take his candy either.

Unfortunately, as you will soon see, I was quickly forced to break this rule. Please don't hold it against me. It was done under duress. I'm really not used to being shot at.

I walked tiredly into the kitchen — which still smelled of smoke — hoping that the strange old man wouldn't take to pounding on the door. I didn't really want to call the police on him — not only would I likely break the telephone in the process (I'm particularly bad with phones) but I really didn't want the old loon carted away in a police car. That would have been —

"Alcatraz Smedry?" a voice suddenly asked.

I jumped, turning from the half-burned cupboard, a box of cornflakes in my hand. A man stood in the doorway behind me, wearing slacks and a button-down shirt. I frowned, realizing that I recognized the symbol on the man's shirt pocket and standard-issue attaché case. He was a foster care caseworker — *this* was the man that Ms. Fletcher had sent to pick me up from the house. I realized that when I'd originally gone chasing the old man up to my room, I'd left the front door open. The caseworker must have come in looking for me while I was upstairs chatting with the lunatic.

"Hi," I said, putting down the box. "I'll be ready in a bit — let me have breakfast first."

"You're him, then?" the caseworker asked, adjusting his horn-rimmed glasses. "The Smedry kid?"

I nodded.

"Good," the man said, then pulled a gun out of his attaché case and raised it toward me. It had a silencer on the barrel.

I froze, shocked. (And don't try to claim that you did anything different the first time a government bureaucrat pulled a gun on you.)

Fortunately, I eventually found my tongue. "Wait!" I said, raising my hands. "What are you doing?"

"Thanks for the sands, kid," the man said, and moved as if to pull the trigger.

At that moment something massive crashed through the wall of my house — something that looked a lot like the front end of an old Model-T Ford. I cried out, dodging to the side, and the caseworker stumbled to the ground in the chaos.

The man who called himself Grandpa Smedry sat happily in the driver's seat. A chunk of smoke-damaged ceiling fell down onto the hood of the car, throwing up a puff of white dust. The old man poked his head out the window.

"Lad," he said, "might I point out that you have two choices right now? You can get in the car with me, or you can stay here with the man holding a gun."

I stood, dazed.

"You really don't have much time to decide," Grandpa Smedry said, leaning toward me, speaking in a kind of half whisper, as if he were sharing some kind of great secret.

Now, I'd like to pause here and note that Grandpa Smedry was lying to me. I didn't have only two choices at that point — I had quite a few more than that. True, I could have chosen to stay in the room and get shot. I also could have chosen to get in the car. However, there were lots of other things I could have done. For instance, I could have run around the house flapping my arms and pretending that I was a penguin. The logical choice to make in this situation would have been to call the police on both of those maniacs.

Unfortunately, I didn't think of penguins or police and instead did as Grandpa Smedry said, scrambling over and getting into the car.

As I stated at the beginning of the chapter, I really shouldn't have done this. I was soon to learn the dangers involved in following strange old men on quests. I don't want to give away any more of the story, but let me say that my fate at this point took a sharp turn toward altars, sacrifices, and evil Librarians.

And possibly some sharks.

The car backed out of the house, the tires leaving tracks in the lawn. I sat in the front passenger seat, still stunned, looking at the wreckage of the Sheldons' house. Bits of siding were falling off the outside wall, crushing Roy's prize tulips. This was more damage than I'd ever done to any foster home. This time it wasn't directly my fault, but . . . well, that didn't change the fact that the kitchen was no longer just burned but also had quite a large hole in it.

We turned onto the street in front of the house — the car puttering along at a modest speed. The caseworker didn't chase after us, but that didn't stop me from watching anxiously until the house disappeared in the distance.

Someone just tried to kill me, I thought, feeling numb. You may find it hard to believe — considering the number of things I'd broken in my life — but this was the first time someone had actually tried to shoot me. It was an unsettling feeling. A little like the way you feel when you have the flu, actually. Maybe there's a connection.

"Well, that was exciting!" Grandpa Smedry said.

I was still staring out the window. The street passed outside, a suburban neighborhood distinctive only in that it looked pretty much like every other one in the nation. Calm two-story houses. Green lawns. Oak trees, shrubs, flower beds, all carefully maintained.

"He tried to kill me," I whispered.

Grandpa Smedry snorted. "Not very well. You'll understand eventually, lad, but pulling a gun on a Smedry isn't exactly the smartest thing a man can do. But that's behind us. Now we have to decide what to do next."

"Next?"

"Of course. We can't just let them have those sands!"

Grandpa Smedry raised a hand and pointed at me. "Don't you understand, lad? It's not just your life that's in danger here. This is the fate of an entire *world* we're juggling! The Free Kingdoms are already losing their war against the Librarians. With a tool like the Sands of Rashid, the Librarians will have just the edge they need to win. If we don't get the sands back before they're smelted — which will only take a few hours — it could lead to the overthrow of the Free Kingdoms themselves! We are civilization's only hope."

"I . . . see," I said.

"I don't think you do, lad. The Lenses smelted from that sand will contain the most powerful Oculatory Distortions either land has ever seen. Gathering those sands was your father's life's work. I can't believe you let the Librarians steal them. I'll be honest, lad — I had higher hopes for you. I really expected better. If only I hadn't come so late . . ."

I sat quietly, looking out the windshield. Now, it's time you understood something about me. Despite what the stories like to say about my honor and my foresight, the truth is that I possess neither trait in large amounts. One trait I've *always* possessed, however, is rashness. Some call it irresponsibility; others call it spontaneity. Either way, I could rightly be called a somewhat reckless boy, not always prone to carefully considering the consequences of my actions.

In this case, of course, there was something more behind the decision I made. I had seen some very odd things that day. It occurred to me that if something as crazy as a gunman showing up in my house could happen, perhaps it could be true that this old man was my grandfather.

Someone had tried to kill me. My house was in a shambles. I was sitting in a hundred-year-old car with a madman. *What the heck,* I thought. *This might be fun.*

I turned, focusing on the man who claimed to be my grandfather. "I . . . didn't *let* them steal the sand," I found myself saying.

Grandpa Smedry turned to me.

"Or, well, I *did,*" I said, "but I let them take the sand on purpose, of course. I wanted to follow them and see what they tried to do with it. After all, how else are we going to uncover their dastardly schemes?"

Grandpa Smedry paused, then he smiled. His eyes twinkled knowingly, and I saw for the first time a hint of wisdom in the old man. Grandpa Smedry didn't seem to believe what I had said, but he reached over anyway, clapping me on the arm. "Now *that's* talking like a Smedry!"

"Now," I said, holding up a finger. "I want to make something very clear. I do not believe a word of what you have told me up to this point."

"Understood," Grandpa Smedry said.

"I'm only going with you because someone just tried to kill me. You see, I am a somewhat reckless boy and am not always prone to carefully considering the consequences of my actions."

"A Smedry trait for certain," Grandpa Smedry noted.

"In fact," I said, "I think that you are a loon and likely not even my grandfather at all."

"Very well, then," Grandpa Smedry said, smiling.

I paused as the old car turned a corner, moving with a very smooth speed. We were leaving the neighborhood behind, turning onto a commercial street. We began to pass convenience stores, service stations, and the occasional fast-food restaurant.

It was at that point that I realized Grandpa Smedry had taken his hands off the wheel sometime during the conversation, and now sat with his hands in his lap, smiling happily. I jumped in surprise.

"Grandpa!" I yelped. "The steering wheel!"

"Drastic Drakes!" Grandpa Smedry exclaimed. "I nearly

forgot!" He grabbed the steering wheel as the car turned another corner. Grandpa Smedry proceeded to turn the wheel back and forth, seemingly in random directions, as a child might play with a toy steering wheel. The car didn't respond to his motions but moved smoothly along the street, picking up speed.

"Good eye, lad!" Grandpa Smedry said. "We always have to keep up appearances, eh?"

"Um . . . yes," I said. "Is the car driving itself, then?"

"Of course. What good would it be if it didn't? Why, you'd have to concentrate so much that it wouldn't be worth the effort. Might as well walk, I say!"

Right, I thought.

Those of you from the Free Kingdoms might be familiar with silimatic engines and can — perhaps — determine how they could be used to mimic a car. Of course, if you're from the Free Kingdoms, you probably have only a vague idea what a car is in the first place, since you're used to much larger vehicles. (It's kind of like a silimatic crawler with wheels instead of legs, though people treat them more like horses. Only, unlike horses, they aren't alive — and when they poop, environmentalists get mad.)

"So," I asked, "where are we going?"

"There's only one place the Librarians would have taken an artifact as powerful as the Sands of Rashid," Grandpa Smedry said. "Their local base of operations."

"That would be . . . the library?"

"Where else? The downtown library, to be exact. We'll have to be very careful infiltrating that place."

I cocked my head. "I've been there before. Last I checked, it wasn't too hard to get in."

"We don't have to just get in," Grandpa Smedry said. "We have to *infiltrate*."

"And the difference is . . . ?"

"One requires far more sneaking." Grandpa Smedry seemed quite delighted by the prospect.

"Ah," I said. "Right, then. Are we going to need any . . . I don't know, special equipment for this? Or, perhaps, some more help?"

"Ah. A very wise idea, lad," Grandpa Smedry said.

And the car suddenly jerked, turning onto a larger street. Cars passed on either side, whizzing off to their separate destinations, Grandpa Smedry's little black automobile puttering along happily in the center lane. Grandpa gave the wheel a few good twists, and we rode in silence.

I kept glancing at the steering wheel, trying to sort out

exactly what mechanism was controlling the vehicle. In my world, vehicles don't drive themselves, and men like Grandpa Smedry are generally kept in small padded rooms with lots of crayons.

Eventually (partially to keep myself from going mad from frustration) I decided to try conversation again. "So," I said, "why do you think that man tried to kill me?"

"Because the Librarians got what they wanted from you, lad," Grandpa Smedry said. "They have the sands, which we all knew would make their way to you eventually. Now that they have your inheritance, you're no longer an asset to them. In fact, you're a threat! They were right to be afraid of your Talent."

"My Talent?"

"Breaking things. All Smedrys have a Talent, my boy. It's part of our lineage."

"So . . . you have one of these Talent things?" I asked.

"Of course I do, lad!" Grandpa Smedry said. "I'm a Smedry, after all."

"What is it?"

Grandpa smiled modestly. "Well, I don't like to brag, but it's quite a powerful Talent indeed."

I raised a skeptical eyebrow.

"You see," Grandpa Smedry said, "I have the ability to arrive late to things."

"Ah," I said. "Of course."

"I know, I know. I don't deserve such power, but I try to make good use of it."

"You are completely nuts, you know." It's always best to be blunt with people.

"Thank you!" Grandpa Smedry said as the car began to slow. The vehicle pulled up to the pumps at a small gas station. I didn't recognize the brand — the sign hanging above the ridiculously high prices simply depicted the image of an upside-down teddy bear.

Our doors swung open on their own. Grandpa hopped out of his seat and rushed over to meet the station attendant, who was approaching to fill up the tank.

I frowned, still sitting in the car. The attendant was dressed in a pair of dirty overalls and no shirt. He was chewing on the end of a piece of straw, as one might see a farmer doing in old Hushlander movies, and he had on a large straw hat.

Grandpa Smedry approached the man with an exaggerated look of nonchalance. "Hello, good sir," Grandpa Smedry said, glancing around. "I'd like a Philip, please."

"Of course, good sir," the attendant said, tipping his hat and accepting a couple of bills from Grandpa Smedry. The attendant approached the car, nodding to me, then took out one of the gasoline hoses and held it up against the side of the car. There was, I noticed, no sign of a gas tank. The attendant stood happily, gas hose pressed uselessly against the side of the car, whistling pleasantly to himself.

"Come, Alcatraz!" Grandpa Smedry said, walking up to the gas station's store. "There isn't time!"

Finally, I just shook my head and climbed out of the car. Grandpa Smedry went inside, the screen door slamming behind him. I walked up, pulled open the screen door — threw the door handle over my shoulder as it broke off — then stepped inside after Grandpa Smedry.

Another attendant — also with straw in his mouth and a large hat on his head — stood leaning against the counter. The small "store" consisted of a single stand of snacks and a wall-sized cooler. The cooler was stocked completely with cans of motor oil, though a sign said ENJOY A COOL REFRESH-ING DRINK!

"Okay," I said, "where exactly are you people finding straw to chew on in the middle of the city? It can't be all that easy to get."

"Quickly, now. Quickly!" Grandpa Smedry gestured frantically from the back of the store. Glancing to either side, he said in a louder voice, "I think I'll have a cool refreshing drink!" Then he pulled open the cooler door.

I froze in place.

Now, it's very important to me that you understand that I am not stupid. It's perfectly all right if you end this book convinced that I'm not the hero that some reports claim me to be. However, I'd rather not everyone I meet presume me to be slow-witted. If that were the case, half of them would likely try and sell me insurance.

The truth is, however, that even clever people can be taken by surprise so soundly that they are at a loss for words. Or, at least, at a loss for words that make sense.

"Gak!" I said.

You see. Now, before you judge me, place yourself in my position. Let's say that you had watched a crazy old man open up a cooler full of oilcans. You would have undoubtedly expected to see . . . well, a cooler full of oilcans on the other side.

You would *not* expect to see a room with a large hearth at the center, blazing with a cheery reddish-orange fire. You would not expect to see two men in full armor standing guard on either side of the door. Indeed, you would not expect to see a room — instead of a cooler full of oilcans — at all.

Perhaps you would have said "Gak" too.

"Gak!" I repeated.

"Would you stop that, boy?" Grandpa Smedry said. "There are absolutely *no* Gaks here. Why do you think we keep so much straw around? Now, come on!" He stepped through the doorway into the room beyond.

I approached slowly, then glanced at the other side of the open glass door — and saw oilcans cooling in their wall racks. I turned, looking through the doorway. It seemed as if I could see much more than I should have been able to. The two knights standing on either side of such a small doorway should have left no room to walk through, yet Grandpa Smedry had passed easily.

I reached out, rapping lightly on one of the knight's breastplates.

"Please don't do that," a voice said from behind the face-plate.

"Oh," I said. "Um, sorry." Still frowning to myself, I stepped into the room.

It was a large chamber. Far larger, I decided, than could

have possibly fit in the store. I could now see a rug set with thronelike chairs arranged to face the hearth in a homey manner (if your home is a medieval castle . . .). To my left, there was a long, broad table, also set with chairs.

"Sing!" Grandpa Smedry yelled, his voice echoing down a hallway to the right. "Sing!"

If he breaks into song, I think I might have to strangle myself . . . I thought, cringing.

"Lord Smedry?" a voice called from down the hallway, and a huge figure rushed into sight.

If you've never seen a large Mokian man in sunglasses, a tunic, and tights before —

Okay. I'm going to assume that you've never seen a large Mokian man in sunglasses, a tunic, and tights. I certainly hadn't.

The man — apparently named Sing — was a good six and a half feet tall, and had dark hair and dark skin. He looked like he could be from Hawaii, or maybe Samoa or Tonga. He had the mass and girth of a linebacker and would have fit right in on the football field. Or, at least, he would have fit right in if he'd been wearing a football uniform, rather than a tunic — a type of garment that I still think looks silly. Bastille has pictures of me wearing one. If you ask her, she'll probably show them to you gleefully.

Of course, if you do that, I'll probably have to hunt you down and kill you. Or dress you in a tunic and take pictures of you. I'm still not sure which is worse.

"Sing," Grandpa Smedry said. "We need to do a full library infiltration. *Now.*"

"A library infiltration?" Sing said excitedly.

"Yes, yes," Grandpa Smedry said hurriedly. "Go get your cousin, and both of you get into your disguises. I need to gather my Lenses."

Sing rushed back the way he had come. Grandpa Smedry walked over to the wall on the other side of the hearth. Not sure what else to do, I followed, watching as Grandpa Smedry knelt beside what appeared to be a large box made entirely of black glass. Grandpa Smedry put his hand on it, closed his eyes, and the front of the box suddenly shattered.

I jumped back, but Grandpa Smedry ignored the broken shards of black glass. He reached into the chest and pulled out a tray wrapped in red velvet. He set this on top of the box, unwrapping the cloth and revealing a small book and about a dozen pairs of spectacles, each with a slightly differ-ent tint of glass.

Grandpa Smedry pulled open the front of his tuxedo jacket, then began to slip the spectacles into little pouches sewn into the lining of the garment. They hung like the watches on the inside of an illegal street peddler's coat.

"Something very strange is going on, isn't it?" I finally asked.

"Yes, lad," Grandpa Smedry said, still arranging the spectacles.

"We're really going to go sneak into a library?"

Grandpa Smedry nodded.

"Only, it's not really a library. But someplace more dangerous."

"Oh, it's really a library," Grandpa Smedry said. "What you haven't realized before is that *all* libraries are far more dangerous than you've always assumed."

"And we're going to break into this one," I repeated. "A place filled with people who want to kill me."

"Most likely," Grandpa Smedry said. "But what else can we do? We either infiltrate, or we let them make those sands into Lenses."

This isn't a joke, I began to realize. *This man isn't actually crazy. Or, at least, the craziness includes much more than just him.* I stood there for a moment, feeling overwhelmed, thinking about what I had seen.

"Well, all right, then," I finally said.

Now, you Hushlanders may think that I took all of these strange experiences quite well. After all, it isn't every day that you get threatened with a gun, then discover a medieval dining room hiding inside the beverage cooler at a local gas station. However, maybe if *you'd* grown up with the magical ability to break almost anything you touched, then you would have been just as quick to accept unusual circumstances.

"Here, lad," Grandpa Smedry said, standing and picking up the final pair of spectacles. They were reddish tinted, like the pair Grandpa Smedry was currently wearing. "These are yours. I've been saving them for you."

I paused. "I don't need glasses."

"You're an Oculator, lad," Grandpa Smedry said. "You'll *always* need glasses."

"Can't I wear sunglasses, like Sing?"

Grandpa Smedry chuckled. "You don't need Warrior's Lenses, lad. You can access abilities far more potent. Here, take these. They're Oculator's Lenses."

"What are Oculators?" I asked.

"We are, my boy. Put them on."

I frowned but took the glasses. I put them on, then glanced around. "Nothing looks different," I said, feeling disappointed. "The room doesn't even look . . . redder."

"Of course not," Grandpa Smedry said. "The tints come from the sands they're made of and help us keep the Lenses straight. They're not intended to make things look different."

"I just . . . thought the glasses would do something."

"They do," Grandpa Smedry said. "They show you things that you need to see. It's just subtle, lad. Wear them for a while — let your eyes get used to them."

"All right. . . ." I glanced over as Grandpa Smedry knelt to put the tray back inside the broken box. "What's that book?"

Grandpa Smedry looked up. "Hmm? This?" He picked up the small book, handing it to me. I opened to the first page. It was filled with scribbles, as if made by a child.

"The Forgotten Language," Grandpa Smedry said. "We've been trying to decipher it for centuries — your father worked on that book for a while, before you were born. He thought its secrets might lead him to the Sands of Rashid."

"This isn't a language," I said. "It's just a bunch of scribbles."

"Well, any language you don't understand would just look like scribbles, lad!"

I flipped through the pages of the book. It was filled with completely random circles, zigzags, loop-dee-loops, and the like. There were no patterns. Some of the pages only had a couple marks on them; others were so black with ink that they looked like a child's rendition of a tornado.

"No," I said. "No, I don't think so. A language has to make patterns! There's nothing like that in here."

"That's the big secret, lad," Grandpa Smedry said, taking back the book. "Why do you think nobody, despite centuries of trying, has managed to break the code? The Incarna people — the ones who wrote in this language — held vast secrets. Unfortunately, nobody can read their records, and the Incarna disappeared many centuries ago."

I wrinkled my brow at the strange comments. Grandpa Smedry stood up, stepping away from the glass box. And, suddenly, the shattered front of the box melted and re-formed its glassy surface.

I stepped back in shock. Then I reached up, suspiciously pulling off my glasses. Yet the box still sat pristine, as if it hadn't been broken in the first place.

"Restoring Glass," Grandpa Smedry said, nodding toward the box. "Only an Oculator can break it. Once he moves too far away, however, it will re-form into its previous shape. Makes for wonderful safes. It's even stronger than Builder's Glass, if used right."

I slipped my Lenses back on.

"Tell me, lad," Grandpa Smedry said, laying a hand on my shoulder, "why did you burn down your foster parents' kitchen?"

I started. That wasn't the question I'd been expecting. "How did you know about that?"

"Why, I'm an Oculator, of course."

I just frowned.

"So why?" he asked. "Why burn it down?"

"It was an accident," I replied.

"Was it?"

I looked away. *Of course it was an accident,* I thought, feeling a bit of shame. *Why would I do something like that on purpose?*

Grandpa Smedry was studying me. "You have a Talent for breaking things," he said. "Or so you have said. Yet lighting fire to a set of drapes and ruining a kitchen with smoke doesn't seem like a use of that Talent. Particularly if you let the fire burn for a while before putting it out. That's not breaking. That seems more like destroying."

"I don't destroy," I said quietly.

"Why, then?" Grandpa Smedry said.

I shrugged. What was he implying? Did he think I *liked* messing things up all the time? Did he think I liked being forced to move every few months? It seemed that every time I came to love someone, they decided that my Talent was just too much to handle.

I felt a stab of loneliness but shoved it down.

"Ah," Grandpa Smedry said. "You won't answer, I see. But I can still wonder, can't I? Why would a boy do such damage to the homes of such kind people? It seems like a perversion of his Talent. Yes, indeed . . ."

I said nothing. Grandpa Smedry just smiled at me, then straightened his bow tie and checked his wristwatch. "Garbled Greens! We're late. Sing! Quentin!"

"We're ready, Uncle!" a voice called from down the hallway.

"Ah, good," Grandpa Smedry said. "Come, my boy. Let me introduce you to your cousins!"

CHAPTER 4

Hushlanders, I'd like to take this opportunity to commend you for reading this book. I realize the difficulty you must have gone through to obtain it — after all, no Librarian is likely to recommend it, considering the secrets it exposes about their kind.

Actually, my experience has been that people generally don't recommend this kind of book at all. It is far too interesting. Perhaps you have had other kinds of books recommended to you. Perhaps, even, you have been given books by friends, parents, or teachers, then told that these books are the type you "have to read." Those books are invariably described as "important" — which, in my experience, pretty much means that they're boring. (Words like *meaningful* and *thoughtful* are other good clues.)

If there is a boy in these kinds of books, he will not go on an adventure to fight against Librarians, paper monsters, and one-eyed Dark Oculators. In fact, the lad will not go on an adventure or fight against anything at all. Instead, his dog will die. Or, in some cases, his mother will die. If it's a *really* meaningful book, both his dog *and* his mother will die. (Apparently, most writers have something against dogs and mothers.)

Neither my mother nor my dog dies in this book. I'm rather tired of those types of stories. In my opinion, such fantastical, unrealistic books — books in which boys live on mountains, families work on farms, or anyone has *anything* to do with the Great Depression — have a tendency to rot the brain. To combat such silliness, I've written the volume you now hold — a solid, true account. Hopefully, it will help anchor you in reality.

So, when people try to give you some book with a shiny round award on the cover, be kind and gracious, but tell them that you don't read "fantasy," because you prefer stories that are real. Then come back here and continue your research on the cult of evil Librarians who secretly rule the world.

"This," Grandpa Smedry proclaimed, pointing to Sing, "is your cousin Sing Sing Smedry. He's a specialist in ancient weapons."

Sing nodded modestly. He had exchanged his tunic for what appeared to be a formal kimono — though he still wore his dark sunglasses. The kimono was of a very rich dark blue silk and, though it fit him quite well, there was something . . . wrong about the entire presentation. More than just the fact that the kimono itself wasn't something a regular person in America wore. Sing's chest parted the front of the silk, and the loose garment hung tied about the waist with a large sash tucked beneath his massive stomach.

"Uh, nice to meet you Sing . . . Sing," I said.

"You can just call me Sing," the large man replied.

"Ask him what his Talent is," Grandpa whispered.

"Oh," I said. "Um, what's your Talent, Sing?"

"I can trip and fall to the ground," Sing said.

I blinked. "*That's* a Talent?"

"It's not as grand as some, I know," Sing said, "but it serves me well."

"And the kimono?" I asked.

"I come from a different kingdom than your grandfather," Sing said. "I am from Mokia, while your grandfather and Quentin are from Melerand."

"Okay," I said. "But what difference does that make?"

"It means I have to wear a different disguise from the

51

rest of you," Sing explained. "That way, I won't stand out as much. If I look like a foreigner to America, people will ignore me."

I paused. "Whatever," I finally said.

"It makes perfect sense," Grandpa Smedry said. "Trust me. We've researched this." He turned and pointed to the other man. "Now, this is your cousin Quentin Smedry." Short and wiry, Quentin wore a sharp tuxedo like that of Grandpa Smedry, complete with a red carnation on the lapel. He had dark brown hair, pale skin, and freckles. Like Sing, he looked to be about thirty years old.

"Well met, young Oculator," Quentin said from behind his dark sunglasses.

"And what is your Talent?" I dutifully asked.

"I can say things that make absolutely no sense whatsoever."

"I thought everyone here had that Talent," I noted.

Nobody laughed. Free Kingdomers never get my jokes.

"He's also really sneaky," Grandpa Smedry said.

Quentin nodded.

"Great," I said. "So, are both of you . . . Oculators?"

"Oh, goodness no," Sing said. "We're cousins to the Smedry family, not members of the direct line."

"Didn't you notice the glasses?" Grandpa Smedry asked. "They're wearing Warrior's Lenses, one of the only kinds of Lenses that a non-Oculator can use."

"Um, yes," I said. "Actually, I did notice the glasses. I . . . noticed the tuxedos too. Is there a reason you dress like that? If we go out like this, we'll kind of stand out, right?"

"Maybe the young lord has a point," Sing said, rubbing his chin.

Lord? I thought. I had no idea what to make of that.

"Should we get Alcatraz a disguise too, Lord Smedry?" Quentin asked my grandfather.

"No, no," Grandpa Smedry said. "He isn't supposed to wear a suit at his age. At least, I don't think . . ."

"I'm fine," I said quickly.

The collection of Smedrys nodded.

Now, many of you Hushlanders may be scoffing at the disguises used by the Smedry group. Before you pass judgment on them, realize that they were somewhat out of their element. Imagine if you were suddenly thrust into a different culture, with very little knowledge of its customs or fashions. Would you know the difference between a Rounsfield tunic and a Larkian tunic? Would you be able to distinguish when to wear a batoled and when to wear a car-foo? Would you even know *where* you wrap a Carlflogian wickerstrap? No? Well, that's because I just made all of those items up. But you didn't know that, did you?

Therefore, my point is proven. All things considered, I think the Smedrys did quite well. I've seen other infiltration teams — ones *without* Grandpa Smedry, who is widely held as the Free Kingdoms' foremost expert on American culture and society. The last group that tried an infiltration without him ended up trying to sneak into the Federal Reserve Bank disguised as potted plants.

They got watered.

"Are we ready, then?" Grandpa Smedry said. "My grandson will be leading this infiltration. Our target is the central downtown library."

Sing and Quentin glanced at each other, looking a bit surprised. Grandpa had mentioned a library infiltration to Sing, but apparently the *downtown* library was not what he'd expected. It made me wonder, once again, what I was getting myself into.

"I realize this will be a most ambitious mission, gentlemen," Grandpa Smedry said. "But we have no choice. Our goal is to recover the legendary Sands of Rashid, which the Librarians have acquired through some very clever scheming and plotting."

Grandpa Smedry turned, nodding to me. "The sands belong to my grandson, and so he will be lead Oculator on this mission. Once we breach the initial stacks, we'll split into two groups and search for the sands. Gather as much information as you can, and recover the sands at all costs. Any questions?"

Quentin raised his hand. "What exactly does this bag of sands *do*?"

Grandpa Smedry wavered. "We don't actually know," he admitted. "Before this, nobody had ever managed to gather enough of them to smelt a Lens. Or, at least, nobody had managed to do it during *our* recorded history. There are vague legends, however. The Lenses of Rashid are supposed to be *very* powerful. They will be a great danger to the people of the Free Kingdoms if they are allowed to fall into Librarian hands."

The room fell silent. Finally, Sing raised a meaty hand. "Does this mean I can bring weapons?"

"Of course," Grandpa Smedry said.

"Can I bring *lots* of weapons?" Sing asked carefully.

"Whatever you deem necessary, Sing," Grandpa Smedry said. "You're the specialist. But go quickly! We're going to be late."

Sing nodded, dashing back down his hallway.

"And you?" Grandpa Smedry asked of Quentin.

"I'm fine," the short man said. "But . . . my lord, don't you think we should tell Bastille what we're doing?"

"Jabbering Jordans, no!" Grandpa Smedry said. "Absolutely not. I forbid it."

"She's not going to be happy. . . ." Quentin said.

"Nonsense," Grandpa Smedry said. "She enjoys being ignored — it gives her an excuse to be grumpy. Now, since we have to wait for Sing to get his weapons, I'm going to go get something to eat. I was clever enough to pack some lunches for myself and the lad. Coming, Alcatraz?"

I shrugged, and we made our way out through the cooler — passing the armored knights — and walked back into the shop. Grandpa Smedry nodded to the two hillbilly attendants, then walked out toward his car, apparently going to grab the briefcases stuffed with food.

I didn't follow him. At that point, I still felt a little overwhelmed by what was happening to me. Part of me couldn't believe what I had seen, so I decided to see if I could figure out how they were hiding that huge room inside. I turned, wandering around to the back of the small service station, then I carefully paced off the lengths of its walls.

The building was a rectangle, ten paces long on two sides, eighteen paces long on the other two. Yet the room inside had been far larger. *A basement?* I wondered. (Yes, I realize that it took me quite some time to accept that the place was magical. You Free Kingdomers really have no idea what it's like to live in Librarian-controlled areas. So, stop judging me and just keep reading.)

I kept at it, trying to figure out some logical explanation. I squatted down on the hot, tar-stained concrete, trying to find a slope in the ground. I stood up, eyeing the back of the building, which was set with a small window. I grabbed a broken chair from a nearby Dumpster, then climbed up to peek into the window.

I couldn't see anything through the dark glass. I pressed my face against it — bumping my glasses against the window — and shaded the sunlight with my hand, but I still couldn't see inside.

I leaned back, sighing. But . . . then it seemed as if I *could* see something. Not through the window, but alongside it.

The edges of the window seemed to fuzz just a little bit, and I got the distinct, *strange* impression that I could see through the wall's siding.

I pulled off my glasses. The illusion disappeared, and the wall looked perfectly normal. I put them back on, and nothing really changed. Yet, as I stared at the wall, I felt the odd sense again. As if I could just *barely* see something. I cocked my head, teetering on the broken chair. Finally, I reached up a hand, laying it against the white siding.

Then I broke it.

I didn't really do much. I didn't have to twist, pull, or yank. I just rested my hand against the wall for a moment, and one of the siding planks popped free and toppled to the ground. Through the broken section, I could see the true wall of the building.

Glass. The entire wall was made of a deep lavender glass.

I saw through the siding, I thought. *Was it my glasses that let me do that?*

A footstep sounded on the gravel behind me.

I jumped, almost slipping off the chair. And there he was: the man from my house, the caseworker — or whatever he was — with the suit and the gun. I wobbled, feeling terror rise again. Of course he would chase us. Of course he would find us. What was I thinking? Why hadn't I just called the police?

"Lad?" Grandpa Smedry's voice called. He appeared around the corner, holding an open briefcase smeared with ketchup. "Your sand-burger is ready. Aren't you hungry?"

The man with the gun spun around, weapon still raised. "Don't move!" he yelled nervously. "Stay right there!"

"Hmm?" Grandpa Smedry asked, still walking.

"*Grandpa!*" I screamed as the caseworker pulled the trigger.

The gun went off.

There was a loud crack, and a chunk of siding blew off the building right in front of Grandpa Smedry. The old man continued to walk along, smiling to himself, looking completely relaxed.

The caseworker fired again, then again. Both times, the bullets hit the wall right in front of Grandpa Smedry.

Now, a true hero would have tackled the man who was shooting his grandfather, or done something else equally heroic. I am not a true hero. I stood frozen with shock.

"Here now," Grandpa Smedry said. "What's going on?"

Looking desperate, the caseworker pointed his gun back at me and pulled the trigger. The consequences, of course, were immediate.

The clip dropped out the bottom of the gun.

The top of the weapon fell off.

The gun's trigger popped free, propelled by a broken spring.

The screws fell out of the gun's sides, dropping to the pavement.

The caseworker widened his eyes in disbelief, watching as the last part of the handle fell to pieces in his hand. In a final moment of indignity, the dying gun belched up a bit of metal — an unfired bullet — which spun in the air a few times before clicking down to the ground.

The man stared at the pieces of his weapon.

Grandpa Smedry paused beside me. "I think you broke it," he whispered to me.

The caseworker turned and scrambled away. Grandpa Smedry watched him go, a sly smile on his lips.

"What did you do?" I asked.

"Me?" Grandpa Smedry said. "No, *you're* the one who did that! At a distance, even! I've rarely seen a Talent work with such power. Though it's a shame to ruin a good antique weapon like that."

"I . . ." I looked at the gun pieces, my heart thumping. "It couldn't have been me. I've never done anything like that before."

"Have you ever been threatened by a weapon before today?" Grandpa Smedry asked.

"Well, no."

Grandpa Smedry nodded. "Panic instinct. Your Talent protects you — even at a distance — when threatened. It's a good thing that he attacked with such a primitive weapon; Talents are much more powerful against them. Honestly, you'd think the Librarians would know not to send someone with a *gun* against a Smedry of the true line. They obviously underestimate you."

"What am I doing here?" I whispered. "They're going to kill me."

"Nonsense, lad," Grandpa Smedry said. "You're a Smedry. We're made of tougher stuff than the Librarians give us credit for. Ruling the Hushlands for so long has made them sloppy."

I stood quietly. Then I looked up. "We're really going to

go *into* the library? The place where these guys come from? Isn't that kind of . . . stupid?"

"Yes," Grandpa Smedry said, speaking — for once — with a quiet solemnity. "You can stay back, if you wish. I know how this must all seem to you. Overwhelming. Terrifying. Strange. But you must understand me when I say our task is *vital*. We've made a terrible mistake — *I've* made a terrible mistake — by letting those sands get into the wrong hands. I'm going to make it right, before thousands upon thousands of people suffer."

"But . . . isn't there anyone else who could do this?"

Grandpa Smedry shook his head. "Those sands will be forged into Lenses before the day is out. Our only chance — the world's only chance — is to get them before that happens."

I nodded slowly. "Then I'm going," I said. "You can't leave me behind."

"Wouldn't dream of it," Grandpa Smedry said. Then he glanced up at the wall where I had broken it. "You do that?"

I nodded again.

"Nagging Nixes! You really *do* have quite the skill for

breaking things," Grandpa Smedry said. "Must have been hard for you when you were younger."

I shrugged.

"What kinds of things can you break?" Grandpa Smedry asked.

"All kinds of things," I said. "Doors, electronics, tables. Once I broke a chicken."

"A *chicken*?"

I nodded. "It was on a field trip. I got . . . kind of frustrated, and I picked up a chicken. When I put it down, it immediately lost all of its feathers, and from then on refused to eat anything but cat food."

"Breaking living things . . ." Grandpa Smedry mumbled to himself. "Extraordinary. Untamed, yes, but extraordinary nonetheless . . ."

I pointed at the building, hoping to change the subject. "It's a glass box."

"Yes," Grandpa Smedry said. "Expander's Glass — if you make space inside of it, you can push out the walls inside without pushing out the walls on the outside."

"That's impossible. It disobeys the laws of physics." (We Hushlanders pay a *lot* of attention to physics.)

"That's just Librarian talk," Grandpa Smedry said. "You've got a lot to learn, lad. Come on, we need to get moving. We're late!"

I allowed myself to be led away, past the three bullet holes in the siding. "They missed," I said, almost to myself. "It's a good thing that man had such bad aim."

Grandpa Smedry laughed. "Bad aim! He didn't have a chance of hitting me. I arrived late to every shot. Your Talent can do some great things, my boy, but it's not the only powerful ability around! I've been arriving late to my own death since before you were born. In fact, once I was so late to an appointment that I got there before I left!"

I paused, trying to work through that last statement, but Grandpa Smedry waved me on. We rounded the building. Quentin and Sing stood with one of the station attendants, talking quietly. Sing had a good dozen different guns strapped to his body. He wore two holsters on each leg, one holster around each upper arm, and one underneath each arm. These were complemented by a couple of uzis tucked into his sash, and what looked like a shotgun tied to his back in a kind of swordlike fashion.

"Oh, dear," Grandpa Smedry said. "He's not supposed to show them off like that, is he?"

"Um, no," I said.

"Could we peace bond them, you think?"

"I don't know what that is," I said, "but I doubt it would help." Still, after getting shot at, the sight of Sing with all those weapons did make me feel a little more comfortable. Until I realized that, if we were going to be bringing an arsenal like that, what would our *enemies* have?

"Ah, well," Grandpa Smedry said. "I already told him he could bring them. We can hide them in a bag or something. They're really not that dangerous — it's not like he's got a sword or something. Anyway, we need to get moving, we're —"

"— late," I said. "Yes, I know."

"Good, then let's —"

At this point, you should be very annoyed with people getting interrupted midsentence. I assure you that I feel the same way. In fact, I think —

A silver sports car screeched into the parking lot. Its windows were tinted the deepest black — even the windshield — and it had a sleek, ominous design, the make and model of which I couldn't quite place. It was like every spy car I'd ever seen melded into one.

The door burst open, and a girl — about my age —

jumped out. Her hair was silvery, matching the car's paint, and she wore a fashionable black skirt and silver jacket, and carried a black handbag.

She appeared to be very, *very* angry.

"Smedry!" she snapped, swatting her purse at Sing as he moved too slowly to get out of her way.

"What?" I asked, jumping back slightly.

"Not you, lad," Grandpa Smedry said with a sigh. "She means me."

"What?" I asked. "What did you do?"

"Nothing much," Grandpa Smedry said. "I just kind of left her behind. That's Bastille, lad. She's our team's knight."

If I'd had any sense, I'd have run away right then.

CHAPTER 5

At this point, perhaps you Hushlanders are beginning to doubt the truth of this narrative. You have seen several odd and inexplicable things happen. (Though, just as a warning, the story so far has actually been quite tame. Just wait until we get to the part with the talking dinosaurs.) Some readers might even think that I'm just making this story up. You might think that everything in this book is dreamy silliness.

Nothing could be further from the truth.

This book is serious. Terribly serious. Your skepticism results from a lifetime of training in the Librarians' school system, where you were taught all kinds of lies. Indeed, you'd probably never even heard of the Smedrys, despite the fact that they are the most famous family of Oculators in the entire world. In most parts of the Free Kingdoms, being a Smedry is considered equivalent to being nobility.

(If you wish to perform a fun test, next time you are in history class, ask your teacher about the Smedrys. If your teacher is a Librarian spy, he or she will get red-faced and give you a detention. If, on the other hand, your teacher is innocent, he or she will simply be confused, then likely give you a detention.)

Remember, despite the fact that this book is being sold as a "fantasy" novel, you must take all of the things it says extremely seriously, as they are quite important, are in no way silly, and always make sense.

Rutabaga.

"*That* is a knight?" I asked, pointing at the silver-haired girl.

"Unfortunately," Grandpa Smedry said.

"But, she's a girl!" I said.

"Yes," Grandpa Smedry said. "And a very dangerous one, I might add. She was sent to protect me."

"Sent?" I said. "Who sent her, then?" *And is she supposed to protect you from Librarians, or from yourself?*

Bastille stalked right up to Grandpa Smedry, placed her hands on her hips, and glared at him. "I'd stab you with something if I didn't know that you'd arrive too late to get hurt."

"Bastille, my dear," Grandpa Smedry said. "How pleasant. Of course I didn't *mean* to leave you behind. You see, I was running late, and I needed to go —"

Bastille held up a hand to silence Grandpa, then glared at me. "Who is he?"

"My grandson," Grandpa Smedry said. "Alcatraz."

"*Another* Smedry?" she asked. "I have to try to protect *four* of you now?"

"Bastille, dear," Grandpa Smedry said. "No need to get upset. He won't be much trouble. Will you, Alcatraz?"

"Uh . . . no," I said. That was, of course, an absolute lie. But would you have said anything different?

Bastille narrowed her eyes. "Somehow I doubt that. What are you planning, old man?"

"Nothing to worry about," Grandpa Smedry said. "Just a little infiltration."

"Of?" Bastille asked.

"The downtown library," Grandpa Smedry said, then smiled innocently.

"*What?*" Bastille said. "Honestly, can't I even leave you alone for half a day? Shattering Glass! What would make you want to infiltrate *that* place?"

"They have the Sands of Rashid," Grandpa Smedry said.

69

"So? We've got plenty of sand."

"These sands are very important," Grandpa Smedry said. "It's an Oculator sort of thing."

Bastille's expression darkened a bit at that comment. She threw her hands into the air. "Whatever," she said. "I assume we're late."

"Very," Grandpa Smedry said.

"Fine." She stabbed a finger at me; I barely suppressed a tense jump. "You, get in my car. You can fill me in on the mission. We'll meet you there, old man."

"Lovely," Grandpa Smedry said, looking relieved.

"I —" I began.

"Must I remind you, Alcatraz," Grandpa Smedry said, "that you shouldn't swear? Now, we're late! Get moving!"

I paused. "Swear?" I said. However, my confusion gave Grandpa Smedry a perfect chance to escape, and I caught sight of the man's eyes twinkling as he jumped into his car, Quentin and Sing joining him.

"For an old man who arrives late to everything," I noted, "he certainly is spry."

"Come on, Smedry!" Bastille growled, climbing back into her sleek car.

I sighed, then rounded the vehicle and pulled open the

passenger side door. I tossed the handle to the side as it broke off, then climbed in. Bastille rapped her knuckles on the dashboard, and the car started. Then she reached for the gear shift, throwing it into reverse.

"Uh, doesn't the car drive itself?" I asked.

"Sometimes," Bastille said. "It can do both — it's a hybrid. We're trying to get closer to things that look like real Hushlander vehicles."

With that, the car burst into motion.

Now, I had been very frightened on several different occasions in my life. The most frightening of these involved an elevator and a mime. Perhaps the second most frightening involved a caseworker and a gun.

Bastille's driving, however, quickly threatened to become number three.

"Aren't you supposed to be some sort of bodyguard?" I asked, furiously working to find a seat belt. There didn't appear to be one.

"Yeah," Bastille said. "So?"

"So, shouldn't you avoid *killing me in a car wreck*?"

Bastille frowned, spinning the wheel and taking a corner at a ridiculous speed. "I don't know what you're talking about."

I sighed, settling into my seat, telling myself that the car probably had some sort of mystical device to protect its occupants. (I was wrong, of course. Both Oculator powers and silimatic technology have to do with glass, and I seriously doubt that an air bag made of — or filled with — glass would be all that effective. Amusing, perhaps, but not effective.)

"Hey," I said. "How old are you?"

"Thirteen," Bastille replied.

"Should you be driving, then?" I asked.

"I don't see why not."

"You're too young," I said.

"Says who?"

"Says the law."

I could see Bastille narrow her eyes, and her hands gripped the wheel even tighter. "Maybe *Librarian* law," she muttered.

This, I thought, *is probably not a topic to pursue further.* "So," I said, trying something different. "What is your Talent?"

Bastille gritted her teeth, glaring out through the windshield.

"Well?" I asked.

"You don't have to rub it in, Smedry."

Great. "You . . . don't have a Talent, then?"

"Of course not," she said. "I'm a Crystin."

"A what?" I asked.

Bastille turned — an action that made me rather uncomfortable, as I thought she should have kept watching the road — and gave me the kind of look that implied that I had just said something very, very stupid. (And, indeed, I had said something very stupid. Fortunately, I made up for it by doing something rather clever — as you will see shortly.)

Bastille turned her eyes back on the road just in time to avoid running over a man dressed like a large slice of pizza. "So you're really *him*, then? The one old Smedry keeps talking about?"

This intrigued me. "He's mentioned me to you?"

Bastille nodded. "Twice a year or so we have to come back to this area and see where you've moved. Old Smedry always manages to lose me before he actually gets to your house — he claims I'll stand out or something. Tell me, did you really knock down one of your foster parents' houses?"

I shifted uncomfortably. "That rumor is exaggerated," I said. "It was just a storage shed."

Bastille nodded, eyes narrowing, as if for some reason

she had a grudge against sheds to go along with her apparent psychopathic dislike of Librarians.

"So . . ." I said slowly. "How does a thirteen-year-old girl become a knight anyway?"

"What's that supposed to mean?" Bastille asked, taking a screeching corner.

And here's where I proved my cleverness: I remained silent.

Bastille seemed to relax a bit. "Look," she said. "I'm sorry. I'm not very good with people. They annoy me. That's probably why I ended up in a job that lets me beat them up."

Is that supposed to be comforting? I wondered.

"Plus," she said, "you're a Smedry — and Smedrys are trouble. They're reckless, and they don't like to think about the consequences of their actions. That means trouble for me. See, *my* job is to keep you alive. It's like . . . sometimes you Smedrys try to get yourselves killed just so I'll get in trouble."

"I'll try my best to avoid something like that," I said honestly. Though her comment did spark a thought in my head. Now that I had begun to accept the things happening around me, I was actually beginning to think of Grandpa Smedry as — well — my grandfather. And that meant . . . *My parents,*

I thought. *They might actually be involved in this. They might actually have sent me that bag of sands.*

They would have been Smedrys too, of course. So, were they some of the ones that "got themselves killed," as Bastille so nicely put it? Or, like all these other relatives I was suddenly learning I had, were my parents still around somewhere?

That was a depressing thought. A lot of us foster children don't like to consider ourselves orphans. It's an outdated term, in my opinion. It brings to mind images of scrawny, dirty-faced thieves living on the street and getting meals from good-hearted nuns. I wasn't an orphan — I had lots of parents. I just never stayed with any of them all that long.

I'd rarely bothered to consider my real parents, since Ms. Fletcher had never been willing to answer questions about them. Somehow, I found the prospect of their survival to be even more depressing than the thought of them being dead.

Why did you burn down your foster parents' kitchen, lad? Grandpa Smedry had asked. I quickly turned away from that line of thinking, focusing again on Bastille.

She was shaking her head, still muttering about Smedrys

who get themselves into trouble. "Your grandfather," she said, "he's the worst. Normal people avoid Inner Libraria. The Librarians have enough minions in our own kingdoms to be plenty threatening. But Leavenworth Smedry? Fighting them isn't *nearly* dangerous enough for him. He has to live as a spy inside of the shattering Hushlands themselves! And, of course, he drags me with him.

"Now he wants to infiltrate a *library*. And not just any library but the regional headquarters — the biggest library in three states." She paused, glancing at me. "You think I have good reason to be annoyed?"

"Definitely," I said, again proving my cleverness.

"That's what I thought," Bastille said. Then she slammed on the brakes.

I smashed against the dash, nearly losing my glasses. I groaned, sitting back. "What?" I asked, holding my head.

"What what?" Bastille said, pushing open the door. "We're here."

"Oh." I opened my door, dropping the inside handle to the street as it came off in my hand. (This kind of thing becomes second nature to you after you break off your first hundred or so door handles.)

Bastille had parked on the side of the street, directly across from the downtown library — a wide, single-story building set on a street corner. The area around us was familiar to me. The downtown wasn't extremely huge — not like that of a city like Chicago or L.A. — but it did have a smattering of large office buildings and hotels. These towered behind us; we were only a few blocks away from the city center.

Bastille rapped the hood of her car. "Go find a place to park," she told it. It immediately started up, then backed away.

I raised an eyebrow. "Handy, that," I noted. Like Grandpa Smedry's car, this one had no visible gas cap. *I wonder what powers it.*

The answer to that, of course, was sand. Silimatic sand, to be precise — sometimes called steamsand. But I really don't have room to go into that now — even if its discovery was what eventually led to the break between silimatic technology and regular Hushlander technology. And that was kind of the foundation for the Librarians breaking off of the Free Kingdoms and creating the Hushlands.

Kind of.

"Old Smedry won't be here for a few more minutes," Bastille said, standing with her handbag over her shoulder. "He'll be late. How does the library look?"

"Umm . . . like a library?" I said.

"Funny, Smedry," she said flatly. "Very funny."

Now, I generally know when I'm being funny. At this moment, I did not believe that I was. I looked over at the building, trying to decide what Bastille had meant.

And, as I stared at it, something seemed to . . . *change* about the library. It wasn't anything I could distinctly put my finger on; it just grew *darker* somehow. More threatening. The windows appeared to curl slightly, like horns, and the stonework shadows took on a menacing cast.

"It looks . . . dangerous," I said.

"Well, of course," Bastille said. "It's a *library*."

"Right," I said. "What else should I look for, then?"

"I don't know," she said. "I'm no Oculator."

I squinted. As I watched, the library seemed to . . . stretch. "It's not just one story," I said with surprise. "It looks like three."

"We knew that already," Bastille said. "Try for less permanent auras."

What does that mean? I wondered, studying the building. It now looked far larger, far more grand, to my eyes. "The top two floors look . . . thinner than the bottom floor. Like they're squeezing in slightly."

"Hmm," Bastille said. "That's probably a population aura — it means the library isn't very full today. Most of the Librarians must be out on missions. That's good for us. Any dark windows?"

"One," I said, noticing it for the first time. "It's jet-black, like it's tinted."

"Shattering Glass," Bastille muttered.

"What?" I asked.

"Dark Oculator," Bastille said. "What floor?"

"Third," I said. "North corner."

"We'll want to stay away from there, then."

I frowned. "I'm guessing a Dark Oculator is something dangerous, right?"

"They're like *super* Librarians," Bastille said.

"Not all Librarians are Oculators?"

She rolled her eyes at me. "Of course not," she said. "Very few people are Oculators. Smedrys on the main line and . . . a few others. Regardless, Dark Oculators are very, very dangerous."

"Well, then," I said. "If I had something valuable — like the Sands of Rashid — then I'd keep them with him. So, that's probably the first place we should go."

Bastille looked at me, eyes narrowing. "Just like a Smedry. If you die, I'm *never* going to get promoted!"

"How comforting," I said, then nodded at the library. "I'm seeing something else about the building. I think . . . some of the windows are glowing just a bit."

"Which ones?"

"All of them, actually," I said, cocking my head. "Even the black one. It's . . . a little strange."

"There's a lot of Oculatory power in there. Strong Lenses, powerful sands, that sort of thing. They're making the glass charge with power by association."

I reached up, sliding the glasses down on my nose. I still couldn't quite tell if I was seeing actual images, or if the light was just playing tricks on me. The changes were so subtle — even the stretching — that they didn't even seem like changes at all. More like impressions.

I pushed the glasses back up, then glanced at Bastille. "You certainly seem to know a lot about this — especially for someone who says she's no Oculator."

Bastille folded her arms, looking away.

"So, how do you know all of this?" I asked. "About the Dark Oculator and the library seeming empty?"

"Anyone would know those auras," she snapped. "They're simple, really. Honestly, Smedry. Even someone raised by *Librarians* should know that."

"I wasn't raised by Librarians," I said. "I was raised by regular people — good people."

"Oh?" Bastille said. "Then why did you work so hard to destroy their houses?"

"Look, aren't knights supposed to be a little less . . . annoying?"

Bastille stood upright, sniffing angrily. Then she swung her purse straight at my head. I started but remained where I was. *The handbag's strap will break,* I thought. *It won't be able to hit me.*

And so, of course, it smashed right into my face. It was surprisingly heavy, as if Bastille had packed a brick or two inside, just in case she had to whack the odd Smedry in the head. I stepped backward — half from the impact, half from surprise — and stumbled, falling to the ground. My head banged against the streetlamp, and I immediately heard a crack up above.

The lamp's bulb shattered on the ground beside me.

Oh, sure, I thought, rubbing my head. *That breaks.*

Bastille sniffed with satisfaction as she looked down at me, but I caught a glimmer of surprise in her eyes — as if she too hadn't expected to be able to hit me.

"Stop making so much noise," she said. "People will notice." Behind her, Grandpa Smedry's little black car finally puttered up the street, coming to a stop beside us. I could see Sing smushed into the backseat, obscuring the entire back window.

Grandpa Smedry climbed perkily out of the car as I stood rubbing my jaw. "What happened?" he asked, glancing at the broken light, then at me, then at Bastille.

"Nothing," I said.

Grandpa Smedry smiled, eyes twinkling, as if he knew exactly what had happened. "Well," he said, "should we be off, then?"

I nodded, straightening my glasses. "Let's go break into the library."

And once again, I considered just how strange my life had become during the last two hours.

Rutabaga.

CHAPTER 6

Kindly pretend that you own a mousetrap factory.

Now, I realize that some of this narrative still might feel a little far-fetched to you. For instance, you might wonder why the Librarians hadn't captured Grandpa Smedry and his little team of spies long before they attempted this particular infiltration. My friends do — as you have undoubtedly noticed — stand out, with their self-driving cars, odd disguises, and near-lethal handbags.

This brings us back to your mousetrap factory. How is it doing? Are profits up? Ah, that's very pleasant.

A mousetrap factory — as you well know, since you own one — creates mousetraps. These mousetraps are used to kill mice. However, your factory is in a very nice, clean part of town. That area itself has never had a problem with mice — your mousetraps are sold to people who live near fields, where mice are far more common.

So, do you set mousetraps in your own factory? Of course not. You've never seen any mice there. And yet, because of this, if a small family of mice *did* somehow sneak into your factory, they might have a very nice time living there, as there are no traps to kill them.

This, friends, is called irony. Your mousetrap factory could itself become infested with mice. In a similar way, the Librarians are very good at patrolling the borders of their lands, keeping out enemy Oculators like Grandpa Smedry. Yet they don't expect to find mice like Grandpa Smedry hiding in the centers of their cities.

And that is why two men in tuxedos, one very large Mokian in sunglasses and a kimono, one young girl with a soldier's grace, and a very confused young Oculator in a green jacket could walk right up to the downtown library without drawing *too* much Librarian attention.

Besides, you've seen the kinds of people who walk around downtown, haven't you?

"All right, Smedry," Bastille said to Grandpa. "What's the plan?"

"Well, first I'll take an Oculatory reading of the building," Grandpa Smedry said.

"Done," Bastille said tersely. "Low Librarian population, high Oculatory magic content, and a very nasty fellow on the third floor."

Grandpa Smedry squinted at the library through his reddish glasses. "Why, yes. How did you know?"

Bastille nodded to me.

Grandpa Smedry smiled broadly. "Getting used to the Lenses this quickly! You show quite a bit of promise, lad. Quite a bit indeed!"

I shrugged. "Bastille did the interpreting. I just described what I saw."

"Was this before or after she smacked you with her purse?" Quentin asked. The short man watched the conversation with amusement, while Sing poked around in the gutter. Sing had, fortunately, put away his weapons — and was now carrying them in a large gym bag, which clashed horribly with his kimono.

"Well," Grandpa Smedry said. "Well, well. Sneaking into the downtown library at last! I think our base infiltration plan should work, wouldn't you say, Quentin?"

The wiry man nodded. "Cantaloupe, fluttering paper makes a duck."

I frowned. "What is that supposed to mean?"

"Don't mind him," Bastille said. "He says things that don't make sense."

His Talent, I thought. *Right.*

"And what, exactly," Bastille said to Grandpa Smedry, "is your base infiltration plan?"

"Quentin takes a few minutes scouting and watching the lobby, just to make sure all's clear," Grandpa Smedry said. "Then Sing makes a distraction and we all sneak into the employee access corridors. There, we split up — one Oculator per team — and search out powerful sources of Oculation. Those sands should glow like nothing else!"

"And if we find the sands?" I asked.

"Take them and get out. Sneakily, of course."

"Huh." Bastille paused. "Why, that actually sounds like a good plan." She seemed surprised.

"Of course it is," Grandpa Smedry said. "We spent long enough working on it! I've worried for years that someday we might have to infiltrate this place."

Worried? I thought. The fact that even Grandpa Smedry

found the infiltration a bit unnerving made it seem even more dangerous than it had before.

"Anyway," Grandpa Smedry said. "Quentin, be off! We're late already!"

The short man nodded, adjusted the carnation on his lapel, then took a deep breath and ducked through the building's broad glass doors.

"Grandfather," I said, glancing at Grandpa Smedry. "These people want to kill me, right?"

"Don't feel bad," he said, removing his Lenses. "They undoubtedly want to kill *all* of us."

"Right," I said. "So, shouldn't we be . . . hiding or something? Not just standing on the street corner in plain sight?"

"Well, answer me this," he said. "That man with the gun — had you seen him before?"

"No."

"Did he recognize you?"

"No, actually," I said. "He asked who I was before he tried to shoot me."

"Exactly," Grandpa Smedry said, strolling over to glance in the library window. "You are a very special person, Alcatraz — and because of that, I suspect that those who watch over you didn't want their peers knowing where you were. You may be surprised to hear this, but there are a lot of factions inside the Librarian ranks. The Dark Oculators, the Order of the Shattered Lens, the Scrivener's Bones . . . though they all work together, there's quite a bit of rivalry between them.

"For the faction controlling your movements, the fewer people who knew about you — or recognized you — the better. That way, they could keep better control over the sands when they arrived." He lowered his voice. "I won't lie, Alcatraz. This mission will be very dangerous. If the Librarians catch us, they will likely kill us. Now that they have the sands, they have no reason to let you live — and every reason to destroy you. However, we have three things going for us. First, very few people will be able to recognize us. That should let us slip into the library without being stopped. Second — as you have noticed — most of the Librarians are out of the library at the moment. My guess is that they're actually searching for you and me, perhaps trying to break into our gas station hideout."

"And the third thing we have going for us?"

Grandpa Smedry smiled. "Nobody would expect us to try something like this! It's completely insane."

Great, I thought.

"Now," he said, "you might want to take off those Oculator's Lenses — they're the only thing that makes you distinctive right now."

I quickly did so.

"Quentin will stay in the lobby and inner stacks for a good five minutes or so — watching for any signs of unusual patterns in Librarian movement or security — meaning we have a little bit of time here. Try to wait without looking suspicious."

I nodded, and Grandpa Smedry wandered over to peek through another window. I lounged with my back against a lamp pole, trying not to break it. It was hard to remain still, considering my anxiety. As I thought about it, the three things Grandpa said we had going for us didn't seem to provide much of an advantage at all. I tried to calm my nerves.

A few moments later, a clink sounded behind me as Sing set down his gym bag of weaponry. I jumped slightly, eyeing the bag — I wasn't really that fond of the idea of having my toes shot off by an "ancient" weapon.

"Alcatraz," Sing said. "Your grandfather tells me that you grew up raised by Hushlander parents!"

"Um, yes," I said slowly.

"Wonderful!" Sing said. "Tell me, tell me. What is the significance of *this*?" He proffered something small and yellow, which he had likely found in the gutter.

"Uh, it's just a bottle cap," I said.

"Yes," Sing said, peering at it through his sunglasses, "I'm aware of your primitive liquid beverage packaging methods. But look, see here. What's this on the *underneath*?"

I accepted the bottle cap. On the underside, I could see printed the words YOU ARE NOT A WINNER.

"See what it says?" Sing asked, pointing with a chubby finger. "Is it common for Hushlanders to print insults on their foodstuffs? What is the purpose of this advertising campaign? Is it to make the consumer feel less secure, so they purchase more highly caffeinated drinks?"

"It's just a contest," I said. "Some of the bottles are winners, some aren't."

Sing frowned. "Why would a bottle want to win a prize? In fact, how do bottles even go about *claiming* prizes? Have they been Alivened? Don't your people understand that Alivening things is *dark* Oculary?"

I rolled my eyes. "It's not Oculary, Sing. If you open the bottle and the cap says you're a winner, then you can claim a prize."

"Oh." He seemed a bit disappointed. Still, he carefully tucked the cap inside a pouch at his waist.

"Why do you care about that anyway?" I asked. "Aren't you an ancient weapons expert?"

"Yes, well," Sing said, "an ancient weapons expert, and an ancient clothing expert, and an ancient cultures expert."

I frowned.

"He's an anthropologist, lad," Grandpa Smedry said from beside the library window. "One of the most famous ones at the Mokian Royal University. That's why he's part of the team."

"Wait," I said. "He's a professor?"

"Of course," Grandpa Smedry said. "Who else would be able to work those blasted guns? The civilized world hasn't used such things for centuries! We figured that we should have someone who can use them — swords might be more effective, but nobody carries them in the Hushlands. It's better to have at least one person on the team who understands and can use local weapons, just to be sure."

Sing nodded eagerly. "But don't worry," he said. "I may not be a soldier, but I've practiced with the weapons quite a bit. I've . . . never shot at something *moving* before, but how difficult can it be?"

I stood quietly, then turned to Grandpa Smedry. "And what about Quentin? Is he a professor too?"

Sing laughed. "No, no. He's just a graduate student."

"He's quite capable, though," Grandpa Smedry said. "He's a language specialist who focuses on Hushlander dialects."

"So," I said, holding up a finger. "Let me get this straight. Our strike team consists of a loony old man, an anthropologist, a grad student, and two kids."

Grandpa Smedry and Sing nodded happily. Bastille, leaning against the library wall a short distance away, gave me a flat stare. "You see what I have to work with?"

I nodded, beginning to understand where she might have gotten such a grumpy attitude.

"Oh, don't be like that," Grandpa Smedry said. He walked over, putting his arm around my shoulders and pulling me aside. "Here, lad, I've got some things I want to give you."

Grandpa Smedry pulled open his tuxedo jacket and removed two pairs of spectacles. "You'll recognize these," he said, holding up a yellow-tinted pair. "I used them back when I first picked you up from the house. They're fairly easy Lenses to wield — if you can already do readings like you did on the library building, you should be able to use these."

I accepted the glasses, then covertly tried them on. At first, nothing changed — but then I thought I saw something. Footsteps, in various colors, fading slowly on the ground around me.

"Tracks," I said with surprise, watching as Sing wandered over to another gutter, leaving a trail of blue footprints on the concrete behind him.

"Indeed, lad," Grandpa Smedry said. "The better you know a person, the longer the footprints will remain visible. Once we get inside, we'll split up — you and I are the only Oculators in the group, and so we're the only ones who will be able to sense where the sands are. But the inside of a library can be deceptively large. Sometimes the stacks form mazes, and it's easy to get lost. If you lose your way, you can use these Tracker's Lenses to retrace your footprints. Also, you can probably track me down, if necessary."

I glanced down. Grandpa Smedry's footprints glowed a blazing white, like little bursts of flame on the ground. I could easily see the trail of white back to Grandpa Smedry's black car, still parked across the street.

"Thanks," I said, still feeling a little apprehensive as I removed and pocketed the Tracker's Lenses.

"You'll do fine, lad," Grandpa Smedry said, picking up a

second pair of glasses. "Remember, this is *your* inheritance we're searching for. You lost it, and you'll have to get it back. I can't hold your hand forever."

I felt like noting that I had seen very little hand-holding in this adventure so far. I didn't really know what was going on, didn't quite trust my sanity anymore, and wasn't even convinced that I wanted my inheritance back. Grandpa Smedry, however, didn't give me an opportunity to complain. He held up the second pair of glasses — they had mostly clear Lenses, with a little dot of red at the center of each one.

"These," he said, handing the Lenses to me, "are one of the most powerful pairs of Oculatory Lenses I possess. However, they're also one of the easiest to use, which is why I'm loaning them to you."

I eyed the glasses. "What do they do?"

"You can use them for many purposes," Grandpa Smedry said. "Once you switch them on — you just have to concentrate a bit to do that — they'll begin gathering the light around you, then direct it out in concentrated beams."

"You mean, like a laser?" I asked.

"Yes," Grandpa Smedry said. "These are *very* dangerous, Alcatraz. I don't carry many offensive Lenses, but I've found these too useful to leave behind. However, let me warn you — if there really is a Dark Oculator in there, he'll be able to sense when you activate these. Only use the Firebringer's Lenses in an emergency!"

Don't get too worried — this isn't the sort of story in which emergencies occur. Yes, it is highly unlikely that you will ever see those Firebringer's Lenses activated. So don't get your hopes up.

I accepted the Firebringer's Lenses from my grandfather, and they immediately started glowing.

"Cavorting Cards!" Grandpa Smedry yelped, dodging to the side as the Lenses blasted a pair of intensely hot beams into the ground just in front of my feet. I hopped backward in shock, nearly dropping the Lenses in surprise.

Grandpa Smedry grabbed the Lenses from behind, deactivating them. The scent of melted tar rose in the air, and I blinked, my vision marked by two bright afterimages of light.

"Well, well," Grandpa Smedry said. "I *told* you they were easy to use." He glanced up at the building. "We should be too far away for that to have been sensed. . . ."

Great, I thought. As my vision cleared, I could see Bastille rolling her eyes.

Sing waddled over, raising his sunglasses and inspecting the three-foot-wide disk of blackened, half-melted concrete. "Nice shot," he noted. "I think it's dead now."

I blushed, but Grandpa Smedry just laughed. "Here," he said, slipping a small velvet bag around the Firebringer's Lenses. He pulled the drawstring tight at the top. "This should keep them safe. Now, with these Lenses and your Talent, you should be able to handle pretty much anything the Librarians throw at you!"

I accepted the glasses back, and fortunately they didn't go off. Now, as I was telling you previously, these Lenses will probably *never* get used in this story. You'll be lucky if you ever get to see them fired. Again.

"Grandfather," I said quietly, eyeing Bastille, then stepping aside again with Grandpa Smedry. "I'm not sure that I can do this."

"Nonsense, lad! You're a Smedry!"

"But I didn't even know I was until earlier today," I said. "Or . . . well, I didn't know what being a Smedry meant. I don't think . . . well, I'm just not ready."

"What makes you say that?" Grandpa Smedry asked.

"I tried to use my Talent earlier," I said. "To stop Bastille from smacking me with her purse. It didn't work. And that wasn't the first time — sometimes I just can't make things break. And when I *don't* want them to break, they usually do anyway."

"Your Talent is still wild," Grandpa Smedry said. "You haven't practiced it enough. Being a Smedry isn't just about having a Talent, it's about finding out how to *use* that Talent. A clever person can make anything turn to his advantage, no matter how much a disadvantage it may seem at first.

"No Smedry Talent is completely controllable. However, if you practice enough, you'll begin to get a grasp on it. Eventually, you'll be able to make things break not just when and where you want, but also *how* you want."

"I . . . ," I said, still uncertain.

"This doesn't sound like you, Alcatraz," Grandpa Smedry said. "Where's that spark of spirit — that stubbornness — that you're always tossing about?"

I frowned. "How do you know what I'm like? You only just met me."

"Oh? You think I've left you in Librarian hands all this time, never checking in on you?"

Of course he checked on me, I thought. *Bastille mentioned something about that.* "But you don't know me," I said. "I mean, you didn't even know what my Talent was."

"I suspected, lad," Grandpa Smedry said. "But I'll admit — I usually got to your foster homes *after* you'd moved somewhere else. Still, I've been watching over you, in my own way."

"If that's the case," I said, "then why —"

"Why did I leave you to the foster homes?" Grandpa Smedry asked. "I'm not that great a parent. A boy needs somebody who can arrive on time to his birthdays and ball games. Besides, there were . . . reasons for letting you grow up in this world."

That didn't seem like much of an explanation to me, but Grandpa didn't look like he'd say more. So, I just sighed. "I just can't help feeling like I won't be much help in this fight. I don't know how to use my Talent, or these Lenses. Maybe I should get a gun or a sword or something."

Grandpa Smedry smiled. "Ah, lad. This war we're fighting — it isn't about guns, or even about swords."

"What is it about, then? Sand?"

"Information," Grandpa Smedry said. "That's the real power in this world. That man who held a gun on us earlier — he had power over you. Why?"

"Because he was going to shoot me," I said.

"Because you *thought* he could shoot you," Grandpa

Smedry said, raising a finger. "But he had no power over me, because I *knew* that he couldn't hurt me. And when he realized that . . ."

"He ran away," I said slowly.

"Information. The Librarians control the *information* in this city — in this whole country. They control what gets read, what gets seen, and what gets learned. Because of that, they have power. Well, we're going to break that power, you and I. But first, we need those sands."

"Grandpa," I said. "You have to have *some* kind of idea what the sands do. You came to get them from me, after all. Didn't you have a plan to use them?"

"Pestering Pullmans, of course I did! I was going to smelt them into Lenses, just like the Librarians are probably doing now. Your father, lad — he was a sandhunter. He spent all his time searching out new and powerful types of sand, gathering the grains together, crafting Lenses like nobody had seen before. The Sands of Rashid were his crowning achievement. His greatest discovery." Grandpa Smedry's voice grew even quieter. "He was convinced they had something to do with where the Smedry family gained its Talents in the first place. The Sands of Rashid are a key, somehow, to understanding the power and origin of our entire family.

Can you understand, perhaps, why the Librarians might want them?"

I nodded slowly. "The Talents."

"Indeed, lad. The Talents. If they could find a way to arm their agents with Talents like ours, then the Free Kingdoms could very well be doomed. Smedry powers are a large part of what has kept the Librarians at bay for so long. But we're losing. The land you call Australia was lost to us only a few decades back — absorbed and added to the Hushlands. Now Sing's homeland has almost fallen. They've already taken some of the outlying Mokian islands — the places you call Hawaii, Tonga, Samoa — and added them to the Hushlands. I fear it will only be a few years before Mokia itself falls."

He paused, then shook his head, looking just a little bit distant as he continued. "Either the Free Kingdoms are going to fall — and everything will become Hushlands — or we're going to find a way to break the Librarians' power. The Smedry Talents, and the secrets these sands will reveal, are key to the next stage of the war. Things are changing . . . things *have* to change. We can't just keep fighting and losing ground. That's why your father spent so much of his life gathering those sands. He felt it was time to go on the offensive."

I felt a stab of anxiety, a question surfacing that I wasn't certain I wanted to know the answer to. Finally, I couldn't keep it down. "Is he still alive, Grandpa?"

"I don't know," he said, looking back at me. "I honestly don't know."

The comment hung in the air. Grandpa Smedry placed a hand on my shoulder. "Alive or not, Attica Smedry was a great man, Alcatraz. An amazing man. And he, like you, was no warrior. We are Oculators. Our weapon is *information*. Keep your eyes, and your mind, open. You'll do just fine."

I nodded slowly.

"Good lad, good lad. Ah, here's Quentin."

The short, tuxedo-wearing man slipped quickly out of the library's front doors. "Five Librarians in the main lobby," he said quietly. "Three behind the checkout desk, two in the stacks. Their patterns are right on schedule with what we've seen from them before. The entrance to the employee corridors is on the far south side. It isn't guarded right now, though a Librarian passes to check on it every few minutes or so."

"All right, then," Grandpa Smedry said. "In we go!"

CHAPTER 7

I seem to recall that last year a Free Kingdoms biographer wrote an article claiming I had spent my childhood performing a "deep infiltration" of Librarian lands. I guess in his mind, spending my life eating Twinkies and playing video games counted as a "deep infiltration."

I hope you Free Kingdomers aren't *too* put out to discover that dragons didn't come and bow to me at my birth. I wasn't tutored by the spirits of my dead Smedry ancestors, nor did I kill my first Librarian by slitting his throat with his own library card.

This is the real me, the troubled boy who grew into an even more troubled young man. Now, I'm not a terrible person. I'm just not a particularly nice one either. If you'd been tied to altars, nearly eaten by walking romance novels, and thrown off a glass pillar taller than Mt. Everest, you might have turned out a little like me yourself.

Sing tripped.

Now, I've seen a lot of people trip in my lifetime. I've seen people stumble, tumble, and misstep. I once saw my foster brother fall down the stairs (not my fault) and I also saw a local bully belly flop when his diving board broke beneath him (I plead the Fifth on that one).

I have never, however, seen a trip quite so . . . well executed as the one Sing performed in the library lobby that day. The hefty Mokian quite convincingly stumbled on the welcome mat just inside the doors. He cried out, hopping on one foot — a teetering, lumbering mound with the kinetic energy of a collapsing building.

People scattered. Children cried, clutching picture books about aardvarks in their terrified fingers. A Librarian raised her hand in warning.

With a weird mixture of skillful grace and a mad lack of control, Sing fell over a comfortable reading chair and collided with a massive bookshelf. Those shelves are — you may know — usually bolted to the floor. That didn't matter. When confronted with a three-hundred-and-fifty-pound Mokian missile, iron bends.

And the bookshelf fell.

Books flew in the air. Pages fluttered. Metal groaned.

"Now's our chance," Grandpa Smedry said. He dashed forward, just one more body in the flurry of lobby activity.

The rest of us followed, scooting past the horrified Librarians. Grandpa Smedry led us behind the children's section, through the media section, and to a pair of shabby doors at the back marked EMPLOYEES ONLY.

"Put your Oculator's Lenses back on, lad," Grandpa Smedry said, sliding on his reddish pair.

I did so as well, and through those Lenses I could see a certain faint glow around the doors. Not a white or black glow, like I'd seen before. But instead . . . a bluish one. The power was focused on a square in the wall. On closer inspection, I could see that that section of the wall was inset with a small square of glass.

"A Hushlander handprint scanner," Grandpa Smedry said. "Kind of like Recognizer's Glass. How quaint. All right, lad, it's your turn."

I gulped quietly, feeling nervous — both because of the Librarians so near and because everyone was counting on me. I reached out and pressed my hand against the door. There was a hum from the glass panel, but I ignored it. Instead I focused on myself.

I'd always known, instinctively, about my power. I'd

always had it, but I'd rarely tried to control it specifically. Now I focused on it, and I felt a tingle — like the shock that comes from touching a battery to your tongue — pulse out of my chest and down my arm.

There was a crack from the door as the lock snapped. "Masterfully done, lad!" Grandpa Smedry said. "Masterfully done indeed."

I shrugged, feeling proud. "Doors have always been my specialty."

Quentin quickly pushed open the door and waved everyone through. Grandpa Smedry's eyes twinkled as he passed me. "I've *always* wanted to do this," he whispered.

I could hear Bastille grumbling something under her breath as she joined us in the hallway, Sing's bag of guns slung over her shoulder. Quentin held the door open for a moment longer, and finally a puffing Sing rounded the bookshelves and joined us.

"Sorry," he said. "One of the female patrons insisted on wrapping my ankle for me." Indeed, his sandal-shod right foot now bore a support bandage.

Quentin closed the door, then checked the handle, twisting it a few times. "Coconuts, the pain don't hurt," he said, then paused. "Sorry," he said, flushing. "Sometimes the gibberish comes out when I don't want it to. Anyway, the lock is still broken — it will be suspicious next time someone comes through here."

"Can't be helped," Grandpa Smedry said, pulling out what appeared to be two small hourglasses. He gave them each a tap, and the sand started flowing. He handed one to me. The sand continued to flow at the same rate no matter which way I turned the device. *Nifty,* I thought. I'd always wanted a magical hourglass.

Well, not really. But if I'd *known* that there were such things as magical hourglasses, I'd have wanted one. Who wouldn't? I should note, however, that the Free Kingdomers would be offended by my calling the hourglass magical. They have very strange feelings on what counts as magical and what doesn't. For instance, Oculatory powers and Smedry Talents are considered a form of magic to most Free Kingdomers, since they are things that can only be performed or used by a few select people. The hourglasses, like the silimatic cars, Sing's glasses, or Bastille's jacket, can be used by anyone. That makes those things "technology" in Free Kingdomer speak.

It's confusing, I know. However, you're probably smart

enough to figure it out. And if you aren't, then I shall likely call you an insulting name. (Wait for Chapter Fifteen.)

"We'll meet here in one hour," Grandpa Smedry said. "Any longer than that, and we'll be getting close to closing time. When that happens, all those Librarians out on patrol will return to check in — and we'll be in serious trouble. Quentin is with me — Sing and Bastille, go with Alcatraz."

"But —" Bastille said.

"No," Grandpa Smedry interrupted. "You're going with him, Bastille. I order you to."

"I'm *your* Crystin," she objected.

"True," Grandpa Smedry said. "But you're sworn to protect *all* Smedrys, especially Oculators. The lad will need your help more than I will."

Bastille huffed quietly but made no further objections. As for myself, I wasn't really sure whether to be annoyed or glad.

"You three inspect this floor, then move up to the second one," Grandpa Smedry said quietly. "Quentin and I will take the top floor."

"But," Bastille said, "that's where the Dark Oculator is!"

"That's where his lair is," Grandpa Smedry corrected.

"That aura glows so brightly because he spends so much time there. You might be able to notice the Dark Oculator's own aura if he's nearby, Alcatraz, but it won't give you much advance warning. Stay quiet and unseen, all right?"

I nodded slowly.

Grandpa Smedry stepped a little closer, speaking quietly. "If you *do* run into him, lad, make certain you keep those Oculator's Lenses on. They can protect you from an enemy's Lenses, if you use them right."

"How . . . how do I manage that?" I asked.

"It takes time to practice, lad," Grandpa Smedry said. "Time we don't have! But, well, it probably won't come to that. Just . . . try to stay away from any rooms that shine black, okay?"

I nodded again.

"Well, then!" Grandpa Smedry said to the whole group. "The Librarians will have to spend ages cleaning up that mess in the lobby. Hopefully, they won't even notice the door until we're gone. One hour! Quickly, now. We're late!"

With that, Grandpa Smedry spun to the left and began walking down the empty white hallway. Quentin waved good-bye. "Rutabaga, fire over the inheritance!" he said, then rushed after the elderly Oculator.

Sing and Bastille turned to me. *It . . . looks like I'm in charge,* I thought with surprise.

This was a strange realization. Yes, yes, I know — Grandpa Smedry had already said that I would have to lead my group. I shouldn't have been surprised to find myself in this situation.

The truth is, however, that I was never the sort of person that people put in charge. Those kinds of duties generally go to the types of boys and girls who deliver apples, answer questions, and smile a lot. Leadership duties do *not* generally go to boys whose desks collapse, who are often accused of playing pranks by removing the doorknobs of school bathrooms, and who once unwittingly made a friend's pants fall down while he was writing on the chalkboard.

I never did manage to get that stunt to work again.

"Um, I guess we go this way," I said, pointing down the hallway.

"You think?" Bastille asked flatly, handing Sing his gym bag of guns. She pulled a pair of sunglasses — Warrior's

Lenses, as the others called them — out of her jacket pocket and slipped them on. Then she took off, walking down the hallway, handbag flipped around her shoulder.

If I ordered her to go back and follow Grandpa instead, I wonder if she'd go. . . . I decided that she probably wouldn't.

"Say, Alcatraz," Sing said as we followed Bastille. "What do you suppose this little wrap on my ankle means?"

I frowned, glancing down. "The bandage?"

"Oh," Sing said. "Is *that* what it is? First aid, it is called, correct?"

"Yes," I said. "Why else would someone wrap your ankle like that?"

Sing glanced down, obviously trying to inspect the ankle bandage while still walking. "Oh, I don't know," he said. "I thought maybe it was some preliminary courtship ritual. . . ." He trailed off, looking toward me hopefully.

"No," I said. "Not a chance."

"That's sad," Sing said. "She was pretty."

"Is that the sort of thing you should be thinking about?" I asked. "I mean, you're an anthropologist — you study cultures. Are you allowed to interfere with the 'natives' you meet?"

"What?" Sing said. "Of course we can! Why, we're *here* to interfere! We're trying to overthrow Librarian domination of the Hushlands, after all."

"Why not just let people live their lives, and live yours?"

Sing looked taken aback. "Alcatraz, the Hushlanders are enslaved! They're being kept in ignorance, living only with the most primitive technologies! Besides, we need to do *something* to fight. Back at the Conclave of Kings, some people are starting to talk about surrendering to the Librarians completely!" He shook his head. "I'm glad for people like your grandfather, people willing to take the fight into Librarian lands. It shows that we won't just sit back and slowly have our kingdoms taken from us."

Up ahead, Bastille glared back at us. "Would you two like to chat a little more?" she snapped. "Perhaps sing a little tune? If there are any Librarians up ahead, we wouldn't want them to miss out on *hearing us coming.*"

Sing looked at his feet sheepishly, and we fell silent — though a part of me wanted to yell something like, "What did you say, Bastille?" as loudly as I could. You see, that is the sad, sorry, terrible thing about sarcasm.

It's really funny.

But I just walked quietly, thinking about what Sing had said — particularly the part about the Librarians only letting Hushlanders have the most "primitive" of technologies. It seemed ridiculous to me that the Free Kingdomers considered things like guns and automobiles to be "primitive." They weren't primitive, they were . . . well, they were what I knew. Growing up in America, I'd come to assume that everything I had — and did — was the newest, best, and most advanced in the world.

It was very unsettling to be confronted by people who weren't impressed by how advanced my culture was. I wanted to huff and think that whatever *they* had must not be all that good either. Except the problem was that I'd *seen* that they had self-driving cars, glasses that could track a person's footprints, and armored knights. All were, in one way or another, superior to what I'd known. (Admit it, knights are just cool.)

I was coming to realize something very difficult. I was slowly accepting that the way I did things — the way my people did things — might not actually be the best way.

In other words, I was feeling humility.

I sincerely hope that you never have to feel this emotion. Like asparagus and fish, it's not really as good for you as everyone says it is. Selfishness, arrogance, and callousness got me much further than humility ever did.

Have I mentioned that I'm not really a very good person?

Our small group reached the end of the unmarked hallway, Bastille still in the lead. She paused, holding up a hand, peeking around the corner. Then she continued onward, her platform sandals making a slight noise as she stepped onto a carpeted floor. Sing and I followed. The room beyond was filled with books.

Really filled.

Perhaps you've never experienced the full, suffocating majesty of a true library. You Hushlanders have probably visited your local libraries — you've perused the parts that normal people are allowed to see. These places tend to have row upon row of neat bookshelves, arranged nicely. They are presented attractively for the same reason that kittens are cute — so that they can draw you in, then pounce on you for the kill.

Seriously. Stay away from kittens.

Public libraries exist to entice. The Librarians want everyone to read their books — whether those books are deep and poignant works about dead puppies or nonfiction books about made-up topics, like the Pilgrims, penicillin, and France. In fact, the only book they *don't* want you to read is the one you're holding right now.

Those aren't real libraries, however. Real libraries take little concern for enticement. You who have visited the basement stacks of a university library's philosophy section know what I'm talking about. In such places, the shelves get squeezed closer and closer together, and they reach higher and higher. Piles of books appear randomly at junctions and in corners waiting to be shelved, like the fourth-generation descendants of a copy of *Summa Theologica* and an edition of *Little Women.*

Dust settles on the books like a gray perversion of rain forest moss, giving the air a certain moldy, unwelcome scent faintly reminiscent of a baledragon's lair. At each corner, you expect to turn and see the withered, skeletal remains of some poor researcher who got lost in the stacks and never found his way out.

And even *those* kinds of libraries are but pale apprentices to the enormous cavern of books that I entered that day. We walked quietly, passing shelves packed so tightly together that only an anorexic racing jockey could have squeezed between them. The bookshelves were easily fifteen feet high, and enormous plaques on the ends proclaimed, in very small letters, the titles each one contained. Long wooden poles with pincerlike hooks leaned against some shelves, and I got the impression that they were used for reaching between the shelves to pull out books.

No, I thought, *it would take a ridiculous amount of practice to learn to do something like that. I must be wrong.*

You may have guessed that I wasn't actually wrong. You see, Librarian apprentices have plenty of time to practice things that are ridiculous. They really only have three duties: First, to learn the incredibly and needlessly complicated filing system used to catalog books in the back library stacks. Second, to practice with the book-hooks. Third, to plot ways to torture an innocent populace.

That third one is the most fun. Kind of like gym class for the murderously insane.

Sing, Bastille, and I crept along the rows, careful to keep an eye out for Librarian apprentices. This was undoubtedly the most dangerous thing I'd ever done in my short life. Fortunately, we were able to get to the eastern edge of the room without incident.

"We should move along the wall," Bastille said quietly, "so Alcatraz can look down each row of books. That way, he might see powerful sources of Oculation."

Sing nodded. "But we should move quickly. We need to find the sands and get out fast, before the Librarians realize they've been infiltrated."

They looked at me expectantly. "Uh, that sounds good," I finally said.

"You've got this leadership thing down, Smedry," Bastille said flatly. "Very inspiring. Come on, then. Let's keep moving."

Bastille and Sing began to walk along the wall. I, however, didn't follow. I had just noticed something hanging on the wall above us: a very large painting that appeared to be an ornate, detailed map of the world.

And it looked nothing like the one I was used to.

CHAPTER 8

At this point, you're probably expecting to read something like, "I suddenly realized that everything I *thought* I had known was untrue."

Though I'll likely use that exact phrase, I should warn you that it is actually misleading. Everything I knew was *not* untrue. In fact, many of the things I'd learned about the world were quite true.

For instance, I knew that the sun came up every day. That was not untrue. (Though, admittedly, that sun shone on a geography I didn't understand.) I knew that my homeland was named the United States of America. That was not untrue. (Though the U.S.A. was not actually run by senators, presidents, and judges — but instead by a cult of evil Librarians.) I knew that sharks were annoying. This also was not untrue. (There's actually nothing witty to add here. Sharks *are* annoying. Particularly the carnivorous kind.)

You have been warned.

I stared up at the enormous wall map and suddenly realized something. Everything I thought I'd known about the world was untrue. "This can't be real. . . ." I whispered, stepping back.

"I'm afraid it is, Alcatraz," Sing said, laying a hand on my shoulder. "That's the world — the entire world, both the Hushlands and the Free Kingdoms. This is the thing that the Librarians don't want you to know about."

I stared. "But it's so . . . big."

And indeed it was. The Americas were there, represented accurately. The other continents — Asia, Australia, Africa, and the rest — were there as well. They were collectively labeled INNER LIBRARIA on the map, but I recognized them easily enough. The difference, then, was the *new* continents. There were three of them, pressed into the oceans between the familiar continents. Two of the new continents were smaller, perhaps the size of Australia. One, however, was very large. It sat directly in the middle of the Pacific Ocean, right between America and Japan.

"It's impossible," I said. "We would have noticed a landmass like that sitting in the middle of the ocean."

"You *think* you would have noticed," Sing said. "But the

truth is that the Librarians control the information in your country. How often have you personally been out sailing in the middle of what you call the Pacific Ocean?"

I paused. "But . . . just because *I* haven't been there doesn't mean anything. The ocean is like kangaroos and grandfathers — I believe that other people have seen it. Ship captains, airplane pilots, satellite images . . ."

"Satellites controlled by the Librarians," Bastille said, regarding the map through her sunglasses. "Your pilots fly guided by instruments and maps that the Librarians provide. And not many people sail boats in your culture — particularly not into the deep ocean. Those who do are bribed, threatened, brainwashed, or — most often — carefully misled."

Sing nodded. "Those other continents make sense, if you think about it. I mean, a planet that is seventy percent water? What would be the point of that much wasted space? I'd *never* have thought people would buy that lie, had I not studied Hushlander cultures."

"People go along with what they're told," Bastille said. "Even intelligent people believe what they read and hear, assuming they're given no reason to question."

I shook my head. "A hidden gas station I can believe, but

this? This isn't some little cover-up or misdirection. There are *three new continents* on that map!"

"Not new," Sing said. "The cultures of the Free Kingdoms are quite well established. Indeed, they're far more advanced than Hushlander cultures."

Bastille nodded. "The Librarians conquered the backward sections of the world first. They're easier to control."

"But . . ." I said. "What about Columbus? What about history?"

"Lies," Sing said quietly. "Fabrications, many of them — the rest are distortions. I mean, haven't you always wondered why your people supposedly developed guns *after* more technology-advanced weapons, like swords?"

"No! Swords *aren't* more advanced than guns!"

Sing and Bastille shared a glance.

"That's what *they* want you to believe, Alcatraz," Sing said. "That way, the Librarians can keep the powerful technology for themselves. Don't you think it's strange that nobody in your culture carries swords anymore?"

"No!" I said, holding up my hands. "Sing, most people don't need to carry swords — or even guns!"

"You've been beaten down," Bastille said quietly. "You're docile. Controlled."

"We're happy!" I said.

"Yes," Sing said. "You're quiet, happy, and completely ignorant — just like you're supposed to be. Don't you have a phrase 'Ignorance is bliss'?"

"The Librarians came up with that one," Bastille said.

I shook my head. "No," I said. "This is too much. I was willing to overlook the self-driving cars. The magic glasses . . . well, they could be some kind of trick. Sneaking into a library, that sounded fun. But this . . . this is ridiculous. I can't accept it."

And likely, you Hushlanders are thinking the very same thing. You are saying to yourself, "The story just lost me. It degenerated into pure silliness. And since only silly people enjoy silliness, I'm going to go read a book about a boy whose dog gets killed by his mother. Twice."

Before you embark upon your voyage into caninicide, I'd like to offer a single argument for your consideration: Plato.

Plato was a funny little Greek man who lived a long time ago. He is probably best known for two things: First, for writing stories about his friends, and second for philosophically proving that somewhere in the eternities there exists a perfect slice of cheesecake. (Read the *Parmenides* — it's in there.) At this moment, however, the reader should be less interested in cheesecake and more interested in caves.

One cave, to be specific. Plato tells a story about a group of prisoners who lived in a very special cave. The prisoners were tied up — heads held so that they could only face one direction — and all they could see was the wall in front of them. A fire behind them threw shadows up on this wall, and these shadows were the only things the prisoners ever knew. To them, the shadows *were* their world. As far as they knew, there was nothing else.

However, one of these prisoners was eventually released and saw that the world was much more than just shadows. At first, he found this new world very, very strange. Once he learned of it, however, he returned and tried to tell his friends about it. They, however, didn't trust him — and didn't want to listen to him. They didn't want to believe in this new world, because it didn't make sense to them.

You Hushlanders are like these people. You have, through no fault of your own, lived your entire life believing in the shadows the Librarians have shown you. The things I reveal in this narrative will seem like nonsense to you. There is no getting around this. No matter how logical my arguments are, they will seem illogical to you. Your mind — struggling to find ways to hold on to your Librarian lies — will think of all kinds of ridiculous concerns. You will ask questions such as, "But what about tidal patterns?" Or, "But how can you explain the lack of increased fuel costs created by airplanes flying around these hidden landmasses?"

Since nothing I can say would be able to pierce your delusions, let the fact that I make *no* arguments stand as ultimate proof that I am right. As Plato once said that his friend Socrates once said, "I know that I'm right because I'm the only person humble enough to admit that I'm not."

Or something like that.

I stood for a long moment, staring up at that map. Part of me — most of me — resisted what I was seeing. And yet, the things I had experienced bounced around in my head, reminding me that many things — like gas station coolers and young men who set fires to kitchens — were not always as simple as they appeared.

"I'll deal with this later," I finally said, turning away from the map. "Let's keep moving."

"Finally," Bastille said. "You Hushlanders. Honestly, sometimes it seems like it would take a hammer to the face to get you to wake up and see the truth."

"Now, Bastille," Sing said as we walked by a long, low

filing cabinet. "That really isn't fair. I think young Lord Smedry is doing quite well, all things considered. It isn't every day that —

"Gak!"

Sing said this last part as he suddenly, and without apparent reason, tripped and fell to the ground. I frowned, looking down, but Bastille burst into motion. She hopped dexterously over Sing, then grabbed me by the arm and threw me to the ground behind the filing cabinet. She ducked down beside me.

"Why —" I began, rubbing my arm in annoyance. Bastille, however, clapped a hand over my mouth, shooting me a very hostile, very persuasive silencing look.

I fell quiet. Then I heard something. Voices approaching.

Bastille removed her hand, then carefully peeked out over the filing cabinet. I moved to do likewise, and Bastille shot me another glance — I could see the glare even through her sunglasses. This time, however, I refused to be cowed.

If she can look, so can I, I thought stubbornly. *I didn't spend thirteen years being a troublemaker so I can get pushed around by a girl my age. Even if she is a pretty good shot with that handbag of hers.*

I peeked over the cabinet. In the distance, moving

between two lines of enormous bookshelves, I could see a group of figures. Most looked like they were wearing dark robes.

"Librarian apprentices," Sing whispered, peeking up beside me. "Doing their tasks. Somewhere in this room, the Master Librarians have placed one misfiled volume. The apprentices have to find it."

I eyed the nearly endless rows of tightly packed bookshelves. "That could take years!" I whispered.

Sing nodded. "Some go insane from the pressure. They're usually the ones who get promoted first."

I shivered as the group moved off. There were a couple of much larger figures following them, and these weren't dressed in robes. They were entirely white, and their bodies moved in a not-quite-natural manner. They lumbered as they stepped, arms held too far to the sides. They trailed behind the Librarian apprentices, moving with ponderous steps, some carrying stacks of books.

I squinted, looking closer. The whitish figures glowed slightly, giving off a dark haze. The apprentices and the white figures turned a corner, disappearing from view.

"What were those?" I whispered. "Those white things that were with them?"

"Alivened," Bastille said, shivering. She glanced at me, standing up. "When Sing trips, Smedry, *always* duck."

"You trip whenever there's danger?"

"Of course not," Sing said. "I only trip when there's danger and when tripping will be helpful. Or, at least, that's usually the way it works."

"Better than your Talent, Oculator," Bastille said with a snort. "Do you want to tell me how you managed to *break* the carpet?"

I glanced down. The carpet lay unraveled around me, separated into individual strands of yarn.

"Come on," Bastille said. "We should keep moving."

I nodded, as did Sing, and we continued along the perimeter of the musty library chamber. We walked in silence; the sight of the apprentices had reminded us of the need for stealth. However, it quickly grew apparent to me that searching through that room wouldn't lead us to the Sands of Rashid. Despite the room's many alcoves (the thousands upon thousands of bookshelves made it feel like a cubicle-filled office for demonic bibliophiles) it didn't seem like the kind of place where one kept objects of great power. I figured that the sands would be in a locked room, or perhaps a laboratory. Not a vast storage chamber.

I spotted a stairwell to the right, and I waved to the others. "We should go up to the second floor."

Bastille raised an eyebrow. "We haven't finished checking this room yet."

"We don't have time," I said, glancing at the hourglass Grandpa Smedry had given me. "This room is too big. Besides, it doesn't feel right."

"We're going to let the fate of the world rest on your feelings?" she asked flatly.

"He *is* our Oculator, Bastille," Sing reminded her. "If he says we go up, then we go up. Besides, he's probably right — the sands aren't likely to be here in the stacks. Somewhere in this building should be a Lens forge. *That's* where they've probably got the sands."

Bastille sighed, then shrugged. "Whatever," she said, pushing past me to lead the way toward the stairs.

I was a little bit surprised that they'd listened to me. I followed Bastille, and Sing took the rear. The stairwell was made of stone, and it reminded me distinctly of something one might find in a medieval castle. It wound in circles around itself and was encased entirely in a massive stone pillar, lit by little frosted windows that let in marginal amounts of daylight.

After several minutes of climbing the steep steps, I was puffing. "Shouldn't we have reached the second floor by now?"

"Space distortion," Bastille said from in front of me. "You didn't honestly expect the Librarians to confine their entire base into a building as small as this one looks?"

"No," I said. "I saw the stretching aura outside. But, I mean, how far up can this stairwell go?"

"As far as it needs to," Bastille said testily.

I sighed but continued to climb. By that logic, the stairwell could go on forever. I didn't, however, want to contemplate that point. "For how 'advanced' you people always claim to be," I noted, "you'd think that the Librarians would have elevators in their buildings."

Bastille snorted. "Elevators? How primitive."

"Well, they're better than stairs."

"Of course they aren't," Bastille said. "It took society *centuries* to develop from the elevator to the flight of stairs."

I frowned. "That doesn't make any sense. Stairs are far less advanced than elevators."

She glanced over her shoulder, looking at me over the top of her sunglasses. I was annoyed to note that she didn't seem the least bit winded.

"Don't be silly," she said. "Why would elevators be *more* advanced than stairs? Obviously, stairs take more effort to climb, are harder to construct, and are far more healthy to use. Therefore, they took longer to develop. Don't you realize how stupid you sound when you claim otherwise?"

"No," I said, annoyed. "The *opposite* is stupid to me. And does everything you say have to sound like an insult?"

"Only when I intend to be insulting," she said, turning and resuming her climb.

I sighed, looking back at Sing, who just shrugged and smiled, still carrying his gym bag of guns. We kept moving.

Stairs are more advanced than elevators? I thought. *Ridiculous.*

Caves. Caves, shadows, and cheesecake.

We eventually reached the top of the stairwell, and it opened out into a long hallway constructed of stone blocks. Along this hallway was a line of large, thick, wooden doors set into stone archways.

"This is more like it," I said. "I'll bet the sands are behind one of these doors."

"Well," Bastille said, "let's try one, then."

I nodded, then walked up to the first door. I listened at it for a moment, but either there was no sound on the other side or the wood was so thick that I couldn't hear anything.

"See any darkness around the door?" Bastille whispered.

I shook my head.

"The Dark Oculator probably isn't in there, then," Bastille said quietly.

"It could open into anything," Sing said.

"Well, we'll never find the sands if we keep to the hallways," Bastille said.

I glanced at the other doors. None of them seemed to glow any more than the others. Bastille was right — we had to start trying them, and any one was as good as the next. So, I took a breath and pushed against the door in front of me. I'd intended to move it open slightly, so we could peek in, but the door swung far more easily than I'd expected. It flew open, exposing the large room beyond, and I stumbled into the doorway.

The room was filled with dinosaurs. Real, live, moving dinosaurs. One of them waved at me.

I paused for a moment. "Oh," I finally said, "is that all? I was worried that I might find something strange in here."

CHAPTER 9

I'd like you to realize two things at this point.

First, I want you to know that when I uttered the words "Oh, is that all? I was worried I might find something strange in here," I wasn't being sarcastic in the least. Actually, I was being quite serious. (Nearly as serious, even, as the moment when I would plead for my life while tied to an altar of outdated encyclopedias.)

You see, after all I'd seen that day, I was growing desensitized to strangeness. The realization that the world contained three new continents still had me in shock. Compared to that revelation, a room full of dinosaurs just couldn't compete.

"Why, hello, good chap!" cried a small green Peteridactyl. "You don't look like a Librarian sort."

Talking rocks might have gotten a reaction out of me.

A talking slice of cheese definitely would have. Talking dinosaurs . . . meh.

The second thing I want you to realize is this: You were warned beforehand about the talking dinosaurs. (Kindly see page 67.) So no whining.

I stepped into the room. It was some sort of storage chamber and was filled with battered cages. Many of those cages contained . . . well, dinosaurs. At least, that's what they looked like to me.

Of course, they were quite different from the dinosaurs I'd learned about in school. For one thing, they weren't very big. (The largest one, an orange Tyrannosaurus Rex, was maybe five or six feet tall. The smallest looked to be only about three feet tall.) The vests, trousers, and British accents were unexpected as well.

"I say," said a Triceratops. "Do you think he's a mute? Does anybody by chance know sign language?"

"Which sign language do you mean?" asked the Pteridactle. "American primitive, New Elshamian, or Librarian standard?"

"My hands aren't articulated enough for sign language," noted the Tyrannosaurus Rex. "That's always been rather a bother for deaf members of my subspecies."

"He can't be mute!" another said. "Didn't he say something when he opened the door?"

Bastille poked her head into the room. "Dinosaurs," she said, noticing the cages. "Useless. Let's move on."

"I say!" said the Triceratops. "Charles, did you hear that?"

"I did indeed!" replied the Pterydactle. "Quite rude, if I do say so myself."

I frowned. "Wait. Dinosaurs are British?"

"Of course not," Bastille said, stepping into the room with a sigh. "They're Melerandian."

"But they're speaking English with a British accent," I said.

"No," Bastille said, rolling her eyes. "They're speaking *Meleran* — just like we are. Where do you think the British and the Americans got the language from?"

"Uh . . . from Great Britain?"

Sing chuckled, stepping into the room and quietly shutting the door. "You think a little island like that spawned a language used by most of the world?"

I frowned again.

"I say," said Charles the Pterrodactlye. "Do you suppose you could let us free? It's *terribly* uncomfortable in here."

"No," Bastille said curtly. "We have to keep a low profile. If you escaped, you could give us away." Then, under her breath, she muttered, "Come on. We don't want to get involved."

"Why not?" I asked. "Maybe they could help us."

Bastille shook her head. "Dinosaurs are *never* useful."

"She certainly is a rude one, isn't she?" asked the Triceratops.

"Tell me about it," I replied, ignoring the dark look Bastille shot me. "Why are you dinosaurs here anyway?"

"Oh, we're to be executed, I'm afraid," Charles said.

The other dinosaurs nodded.

"What did you do?" I asked. "Eat somebody important?"

Charles gasped. "No, no. That's a Librarian myth, good sir. We don't eat people. Not only would that be barbaric of us, but I'm sure you would taste terrible! Why, all we did was come to your continent for a visit!"

"Stupid creatures," Bastille said, leaning against the door. "Why would you visit the Hushlands? You know that the Librarians have built you up as mythological monsters."

"Actually," Sing noted, "I believe the Librarians claim that dinosaurs are extinct."

"Yes, yes," Charles said. "Quite true. That's why they're going to execute us! Something about enlarging our bones, then putting them inside of rock formations, so that they can be dug out by human archaeologists."

"Terribly undignified!" the T. Rex said.

"Why did you even come here?" Sing asked. "The Hushlands aren't the type of place one comes on vacation."

The dinosaurs exchanged ashamed glances.

"We . . . wanted to write a paper," Charles admitted. "About life in the Hushlands."

"Oh, for the love of . . ." I said. "Is *everybody* from your continent a professor?"

"We're not professors," the T. Rex huffed.

"We're field researchers," Charles said. "Completely different."

"We wanted to study primitives in their own environment," the Triceratops said. Then he squinted, looking up at Sing. "I say, don't I recognize you?"

Sing smiled modestly. "Sing Smedry."

"Why, it *is* you!" the Triceratops said. "I absolutely *loved* your paper on Hushlander bartering techniques. Do they really trade little books in exchange for goods?"

"They call the books 'dollar bills,'" Sing said. "They're

each only one page long — and yes, they do use them as currency. What else would you expect from a society constructed by Librarians?"

"Can we go?" Bastille asked, looking tersely at me.

"What about freeing us?" the Triceratops asked. "It would be terribly kind of you. We'll be quiet. We know how to sneak."

"We're quite good at blending in," Charles agreed.

"Oh?" Bastille asked, raising an eyebrow. "And how long did you last on this continent before being captured?"

"Uh . . ." Charles began.

"Well," the T. Rex said. "We *did* get spotted rather quickly."

"Shouldn't have landed on such a popular beach," the Triceratops agreed.

"We pretended to be dead fish that washed up with the tide," Charles said. "That didn't work very well."

"I kept sneezing," said the T. Rex. "Blasted seaweed always makes me sneeze."

I glanced at Bastille, then back at the dinosaurs. "We'll come back for you," I told them. "She's right — we can't risk exposing ourselves right now."

"Ah, very well, then," said Charles the Pterradactyl. "We'll just sit here."

"In our cages," said the T. Rex.

"Contemplating our impending doom," said the Triceratops.

The reader may wonder why one of the dinosaurs was consistently referred to by his first name, while the others were not. There is a very simple and understandable reason for this.

Have you ever tried to spell *Pterodactyl*?

We slipped out of the dinosaur room. "Talking dino-saurs," I mumbled.

Bastille nodded. "I can only think of one group more annoying."

I raised an eyebrow.

"Talking rocks," she said. "Where do we go next?"

"Next door." I pointed down the hallway.

"Any auras?" Bastille asked.

"No," I replied.

"That doesn't necessarily mean the sands won't be in there," Bastille said. "It would take some time for the sands to charge the area with a glow. I think we should check them."

I nodded. "Sounds good."

"Let me open this one," Bastille said. "If there *is*

something dangerous in there, it would be better if you didn't just stumble in and stare at it with a dumb look."

I flushed as Bastille waved Sing and me back. Then she crept up to the door, placing her ear against the wood.

I turned to Sing. "So . . . do you really have talking rocks in your world?"

"Oh, yes," he said with a nod.

"That must be odd," I said contemplatively. "Talking rocks . . ."

"They're really not all that exciting," Sing said.

I looked at him quizzically.

"Can you honestly imagine anything interesting that a rock might have to say?" Sing asked.

Bastille shot an annoyed look back at us, and we quieted. Finally, she shook her head. "Can't hear anything," she whispered, moving to push open the door.

"Wait," I said, an idea occurring to me. I pulled out the yellow-tinted Tracker's Lenses and slid them on. After focusing, I could see Bastille's footprints on the stone — they glowed a faint red. Other than that, the hallway was empty of footprints, except for mine and Sing's.

"Nobody's gone in the room recently," I said. "Should be safe."

Bastille cocked her head, a strange expression on her face. As if she were surprised to see me do something useful. Then she quietly cracked the door open, peeking through the slit. After a moment she pushed it open the rest of the way, waving Sing and me forward.

Instead of dinosaur cages, this room held bookshelves. They weren't the towering, closely packed bookshelves of the first floor, however. These were built into the walls and made the room look like a comfortable den. There were three desks in the room, all unoccupied, though all of them had books open on top of them.

Bastille shut the door behind us. I glanced around the small den — it was well furnished and, despite the books, didn't feel cluttered. *This is more like it,* I thought. *This is the kind of place I might stash something important.*

"Quickly," Bastille said. "See what you can find."

Sing immediately walked to one of the desks. Bastille began poking around, peeking behind paintings, probably looking for a hidden safe. I stood for a moment, then walked over to the bookshelves.

"Smedry," Bastille hissed from across the room.

I glanced over at her.

She tapped her dark sunglasses. Only then did I realize

that I was still wearing the Tracker's Lenses. I quickly swapped them for my Oculator's Lenses, then stepped back, trying to get a good view of the room.

Nothing glowed distinctly. The books, however . . . the text on the spines seemed to *wiggle* slightly. I frowned, walking over to a shelf and pulling off one of the volumes. The text had stopped wiggling, but I couldn't read it anyway.

It was just like the book in Grandpa Smedry's glass safe. The pages were filled with scribbles, like a child had taken a fountain pen to a sheet of paper and attacked it in a bout of infantile artistic wrath. There was no specific direction, or reason, to the lines.

"These books," I said. "Grandpa Smedry has one like them in the gas station."

"The Forgotten Language," Sing said from the other side of the room. "It doesn't look like the Librarians are having any luck deciphering it either. Look."

Bastille and I walked over to the place where Sing was sitting. There, set out on the table, were pages and pages of scratches and scribbles. Beside them were different combinations of English letters, obviously written by someone trying to make sense of the scribbles.

"What would happen if they *did* translate it?" I asked.

Sing snorted. "I wish them good luck. Scholars have been trying to do *that* for centuries."

"But why?" I asked.

"Because," Sing said. "Isn't it obvious? There are important things hidden in those Forgotten Language texts. If that weren't the case, the language wouldn't have been forgotten."

I frowned. Something about that didn't make sense. "It seems the opposite to me," I said. "If the language were all that important, then we wouldn't have forgotten it, would we?"

Both of them looked at me as if I were crazy.

"Alcatraz," Sing said. "The Forgotten Language wasn't just accidentally forgotten. We were *made* to forget it. The entire world somehow lost the ability to read it some three thousand years back. Nobody knows how it happened, but the Incarna — the people who wrote all of these texts — decided that the world wasn't worthy of their knowledge. We forgot all of it, as well as the method of reading their language."

"Don't they teach you anything in those schools of yours?" Bastille said, not for the first time.

I gave her a flat look. "Librarian schools? What do you expect?"

She shrugged, glancing away.

Sing glanced at me. "It's taken us three thousand years to get back even a fraction of the knowledge we had before the Incarna stole it from us. But, there are still lots of things we've never discovered. And nobody has been able to crack the code of the Forgotten Language despite three thousand years of work."

The room fell silent. Finally, Bastille glanced at me. "Well?"

"Well what?" I asked.

She glanced at me over the top of her sunglasses, giving me a suffering look. "The Sands of Rashid. Are they in here?"

"Oh," I said. "I don't see anything glowing."

"Good enough. You would be able to see them glowing even if they were encased in Rebuilder's Glass."

"I did notice something odd, though," I said, glancing back at the bookshelves. "The scribbles on the spines of those books started to wiggle the first time I looked at them."

Bastille nodded. "That's just an attention aura — the glasses were trying to get you to notice the text."

"The *glasses* wanted me to notice something?" I asked.

"Well," Bastille said. "More like your subconscious wanted you to notice something. The glasses aren't alive, they just help you focus. I'd guess that because you've seen the Forgotten Language before, your subconscious recognized it on those spines. So, the glasses gave you an attention aura to make you notice."

"Interesting," Sing said.

I nodded slowly — then, curiously, Bastille's entire shape fuzzed just slightly. Another attention aura? If so, what was it I was supposed to notice about her?

How do you know so much about Oculator auras, Bastille? I thought, realizing what was bothering me. There was more to this girl than she liked to let people see.

Some things just weren't making sense to me. Why was Bastille chosen to protect Grandpa Smedry? Certainly, she seemed like a force to be reckoned with — but she was still just a kid. And for her to know so much about Oculating, when Sing — a professor, and a Smedry to boot — didn't seem to know much . . .

Well, it was odd.

You may think those above paragraphs are some kind of foreshadowing. You're right. Of course, those thoughts weren't foreshadowing when they occurred to me. I couldn't know that they'd be important.

I tend to have a lot of ridiculous thoughts. I'm having some right now. Most of these certainly *aren't* important. And so, I usually only mention the ones that matter. For instance, I could have told you that many of the lanterns in the library looked like types of fruits and vegetables. But that has no real relevance to the plot, so I left it out. Likewise, I could have included the scene where I noticed the roots of Bastille's hair and wondered why she dyed it silver, rather than letting it grow its natural red. But since that part isn't relevant to the —

Oh. Wait. Actually, that *is* relevant. Never mind.

"Ready to go, then?" Bastille asked.

"I'm taking these," Sing said. He unzipped his duffel bag, tossed aside a spare uzi, then stuffed in the translators' notes. "Quentin would kill me if I left them behind."

"Here," I said, tossing a Forgotten Language book into the bag. "Might as well take one of these for him too."

"Good idea," Sing said, zipping up his duffel.

"There's just one thing I don't get," I said.

"*One* thing?" Bastille asked with a snort.

"Why do the Librarians work so hard to keep everything quiet?" I asked. "Why go to all that trouble? What's the point?"

"Do you have to have a point if you're an evil sect of Librarians?" Bastille asked with annoyance.

I fell silent.

"They do have a point, Bastille," Sing said. "Everyone has a reason to do what they do. The Librarians, they were founded by a man named Biblioden. Most people just call him The Scrivener. He taught that the world is too strange a place — that it needs to be ordered, organized, and controlled. One of Biblioden's teachings is the Fire Metaphor. He pointed out that if you let fire burn free, it destroys everything around it. If you contain it, however, it can be very useful. Well, the Librarians think that other things — Oculatory powers, technology, Smedry Talents — need to be contained too. Controlled."

"Controlled by those who supposedly know better," Bastille said. "Librarians."

"So," I said, "all of this cover-up . . ."

"It's to create the world The Scrivener envisioned," Sing said. "To create a place where information is carefully controlled by a few select people, and where power is in the hands of his followers. A world where nothing strange or abnormal exists. Where magic is derided, and everything can be blissfully ordinary."

And that's what we fight, I thought, coming to understand for the first time. *That's what this is all about.*

Sing threw his duffel over his shoulder, adjusting his glasses as Bastille went back to the door, cracking it open to make certain nobody was in the hallway. As she did, I noticed the discarded uzi, lying ignored on the floor. Trying to look nonchalant, I wandered over to it, absently reaching down and picking it up.

This is, I would like to note, precisely the same thing *any* thirteen-year-old boy would do in that situation. A boy who wouldn't do such a thing probably hasn't been reading enough books about killer Librarians.

Unfortunately for me, I wasn't like most thirteen-year-old boys. I was special. And, in this case, my specialness manifested itself by making the gun break the moment I touched it. The weapon made a noise almost like a sigh, then busted into a hundred different pieces. Bullets rolled away like marbles, leaving me sullenly holding a piece of the gun's grip.

"Oh," Sing said. "I meant to leave that there, Alcatraz."

"Yes, well," I said, dropping the scrap of metal. "I thought I should . . . uh, take care of the gun, just in case. We wouldn't want anyone to find such a primitive weapon and hurt themselves by accident."

"Ah, good idea," Sing said. Bastille held open the door, then we all moved into the hallway.

"Next door," Bastille said.

I nodded, switching glasses. As soon as the Tracker's Lenses were on, I noticed something: bright black footprints, burning on the ground.

They were still fresh — I could see the trail disappearing as I watched. And there was a certain . . . *power* to the footprints. I instantly knew to whom they belonged.

The footprints passed through the hallway, beside a yellowish-black set, disappearing into the distance. They burned, foreboding and dark, like gasoline dripped to the floor and lit with black fire.

As Bastille crept toward the next door in the hallway, I made a decision. "Forget the room," I said, growing tense. "Follow me!"

CHAPTER 10

Are you annoyed with me yet?

Good. I've worked very hard — perhaps I will explain why later — to frustrate you. One of the ways I do this is by leaving cliff-hangers at the ends of chapters. These sorts of things force you, the reader, to keep on plunging through my story.

This time, at least, I plan to make good on the cliff-hanger. The one at the end of the previous chapter is entirely different from the hook I used at the beginning of the book. You remember that one, don't you? Just in case you've forgotten, I believe it said:

"So, there I was, tied to an altar made from outdated encyclopedias, about to get sacrificed to the dark powers by a cult of evil Librarians."

This sort of behavior — using hooks to start books — is inexcusable. In fact, when you read a sentence like that one at the beginning of a book, you should know *not* to continue reading. I have it on good authority that when an author gives a hook like this, he isn't ever likely to explain why the poor hero is tied to an altar — and, if the explanation *does* come, it won't arrive until the end of the story. You'll have to sit through long, laborious essays, wandering narratives, and endless ponderings before you reach the small bit of the story that you *wanted* to read in the first place.

Hooks and cliff-hangers belong only at the ends of chapters. That way, the reader moves on directly to the next page — where, thankfully, they can read more of the story without having to suffer some sort of mindless interruption.

Honestly, authors can be so self-indulgent.

"Alcatraz?" Bastille asked as I took off down the hallway following the footprints.

I waved for her to follow. The black footprints were fading quickly. True, if the black ones disappeared, we could just follow the yellow ones, since they appeared more stable. But if I didn't keep up with the black ones, I wouldn't know if the two sets diverged.

Bastille and Sing hurried along behind me. As we moved, however, the thought of what I was doing finally hit me: I was chasing down the Dark Oculator. I didn't even really know what a Dark Oculator was, but I was pretty certain that I didn't want to meet one. This was, after all, probably the person who had sent a gunman to kill me.

Yet I was also pretty certain that this Dark Oculator was the leader of the library. The most important person around. That made him the person most likely to know where the Sands of Rashid were. And I intended to get those sands back. They were my link to my parents, perhaps the only clue I would ever get to help me know what had happened to them. So, I kept moving.

Now, some of you reading this may assume that I was being brave. In truth, my insides were growing sick at the thought of what I was doing. My only excuse can be that I didn't really understand how much danger I was in. Knowledge of the Free Kingdoms and Oculators was still new to me, and the threat didn't quite seem real.

If I'd understood the risk — the death and pain that pursuing this course would lead to — I would have turned back right then. And it would have been the right decision, despite what my biographers say. You'll see.

"What are we doing?" Bastille hissed, walking quickly beside me.

"Footprints," I whispered. "Someone passed this way a short time ago."

"So?" she asked.

"They're black."

Bastille stopped short, falling behind. She hurriedly caught up, though. "*How* black?"

"I don't know," I said. "Blackish black."

"But I mean . . ."

"It's him," I said. "The footprints seem like they're . . . *burning*. Like they were seared into the stones and are slowly melting away the floor. That's how black they are."

"That's the Dark Oculator, then," Bastille said. "We don't want to follow them."

"Of course we do. We have to find the sands!"

Bastille grabbed my arm, yanking me to a halt. Sing puffed up behind us. "Goodness!" he said. "Ancient weapons certainly are heavy!"

"Bastille," I said, "we're going to lose the trail!"

"Smedry, *listen to me*," she said, still gripping my arm. "Your grandfather might be able to face a high-level Dark Oculator. *Might.* And he's one of the Free Kingdoms' most powerful living Oculators, with an entire repertoire of Lenses. What do you have? Two pairs?"

Three, I thought, reaching into my jacket pocket. *Those Firebringer's Lenses. If I could turn them on the Dark Oculator . . .*

"I know that look," Bastille said. "Your grandfather gets it too. Shattering Glass, Smedry! Is everyone in your family an idiot? Do your Talent genes replace the ones that give most people common sense? How am I supposed to protect you if you insist on being so foolish?"

I hesitated. Down the hallway, the last of the dark footprints burned away, leaving only the yellowish set. I looked down at them, frowning to myself.

I'm missing something, I thought.

Grandpa Smedry had explained about the Tracker's Lenses. He'd said . . . that the footprints would remain longer for people that I knew well. I glanced back down the way we had come. My own footprints, glowing a weak white, showed no signs of fading. Bastille and Sing's sets, however, were already beginning to disappear.

That yellow set of footprints, I realized, turning back toward the way the Dark Oculator had gone. *They must belong to someone I know. . . .*

That was too big a mystery for me to ignore.

I reached into my pocket, pulling out the small hour-glass Grandpa Smedry had given me. "Look, Bastille," I said, holding it up before her. "We only have a *half hour* until this place gets filled with Librarians back from patrolling. If that happens, we'll get caught, and those sands will fall permanently into Librarian hands. We don't have time to go poking around, looking in random doors. This place is *way* too big. There's only one way to find what we need."

"The Dark Oculator might not even have the sands with him," Bastille said.

"Perhaps," I said. "But he might know where to find them — or he might lead us to them. We at least have to try to follow him. It's our best lead."

Bastille nodded reluctantly. "Don't try to fight him, though."

"I won't," I said. "Don't worry — it'll be all right."

And if you believe that, then I have a bridge to sell you . . . *on the moon.*

To my credit, I didn't really *want* to face down a Dark Oculator. I was half hoping that Bastille would talk me out of the decision. Usually when I tried to do reckless things, there had been adults around to stop me. But things were different now. By some act of fortune — perhaps even more strange than the appearance of talking dinosaurs and evil Librarians — I was in charge. And people listened to me. I was realizing that if I chose poorly, I would not only get myself into trouble but I might end up getting Bastille and Sing hurt as well.

It was a sobering thought. My life was changing, and so my view of myself had to change as well. You might think I was turning into a hero — however, the truth is that I was just setting myself up for an even greater fall.

"We'll stay out of sight," I said. "Eavesdrop and hope the Dark Oculator mentions where the sands are. Our goal is *not* to fight him. At the first sign of trouble — or, in Sing's case, tripping — we'll back out. All right?"

Bastille and Sing nodded. Then I turned. The yellowish footprints were still there. A little more cautious, I followed them down the hallway. We passed a couple more archways, set with solid wooden doors, but the footprints didn't lead into any of them. The hallway led deeper and deeper into the library.

Why build a library that looks like a castle inside? I thought, passing an ornate lantern bracket shaped like a cantaloupe.

The lantern atop it burned a large flame, and — despite the tense situation — something occurred to me.

"Fire," I said as we walked.

"What?" Bastille asked.

"You can't tell me that those lanterns are more 'advanced' than electric lights."

"You're still worried about *that*?"

I shrugged as we paused at an intersection, and Bastille peeked around it, then waved the all clear.

"They just don't seem very practical to me," I whispered as we started again. "You can turn electric lights on and off with a switch."

"You can do that with these too," Bastille said. "Except without the switch."

I frowned. "Uh . . . okay."

"Besides," Bastille whispered. "You can light things on fire with these lamps. Can you do that with electric ones?"

"Well, not most of them," I said, pointing as the footprints turned down a side corridor. "But that's sort of the idea. Open flames like that can burn things down."

I couldn't see because of the sunglasses, but I had the distinct impression that Bastille was rolling her eyes at me. "They only burn things if you *want* them to, Smedry."

"How does *that* work?" I whispered, frowning.

"Look, do we have time for this?" Bastille asked.

"Actually, no," I said. "Look up there."

I pointed ahead, toward a place where the hallway opened into a large room. This diversion was actually quite fortunate for Bastille, for it meant that she didn't have to explain how silimatic lanterns work — something I now know that she couldn't have done anyway. Not that I'd point out her ignorance to her directly. She tends to start swinging handbags whenever I do things like that.

Bastille went up the hallway first. Despite myself, I was impressed by her stealth as she crept forward, close to the wall. The room ahead was far better lit than the hallway, and her movements threw shadows back along the walls. After reaching the place where the hallway opened into the room, she waved Sing and me forward. I realized that I could hear voices up ahead.

I approached as quietly as possible, creeping up next to Bastille. There was a quiet clink as Sing huddled beside us, setting down his gym bag. Bastille shot him a harsh look, and he shrugged apologetically.

The room at the end of the corridor was actually a large,

three-story entryway. It was circular, and our corridor opened up onto a second-story balcony overlooking the main floor down below. The footprints turned and wound around a set of stairs, leading down. We inched forward to the edge of the balcony and looked down upon the people I had tracked.

One of them was indeed a person I knew. It was a person I had known for my entire life: Ms. Fletcher.

It made sense. After all, Grandpa Smedry had said that she'd been the one to steal the sands from my room. The idea had seemed silly to me at the time, but then a lot of things had been confusing to me back then. I could now see that he must have been right.

And yet, it seemed so odd to see a person from my regular life in the middle of the library. Ms. Fletcher wasn't a friend, but she was one of the few constants in my life. She had directed my moves from foster family to foster family, always checking in on me, looking after me. . . .

Spying on me?

Ms. Fletcher still wore her unflattering black skirt, tight bun, and horn-rimmed glasses. She stood next to a hefty man in a dark business suit with a black shirt and a red power tie. As he turned, conversing with Ms. Fletcher, I could see that he wore a patch over one eye. The other eye held a red-tinted monocle.

Bastille breathed in sharply.

"What?" I asked quietly.

"He only has one eye," she said. "I think that's Radrian Blackburn. He's a very powerful Oculator, Alcatraz — they say he put out his own eye to increase the power focused through his single remaining one."

I frowned. "Blackburn?" I whispered. "That's an interesting name."

"It's a mountain," Bastille said. "I think in the state you call Alaska. Librarians named mountains after themselves — just like they named prisons after us."

I cocked my head. "I'm pretty sure that Alcatraz Island is older than I am, Bastille."

"You were named after someone, Alcatraz," Sing said, crawling up next to us. "A famous Oculator from long ago. Among people from our world — and among our opponents — names tend to get reused. We're traditional that way."

I leaned forward. Blackburn didn't look all that threatening. True, he had an arrogant voice and seemed a bit imposing in his black-on-black suit. Still, I had expected something more dramatic. A cape, maybe?

I was, of course, missing something very important. You'll see in a moment.

Beside me, Bastille looked *very* nervous. I could see her pulling her purse up, reaching one hand inside of it. An odd gesture, I thought, since I doubted there was anything inside that purse that could face down a Dark Oculator. Anyway, the voices from below quickly stole my attention. I could just barely hear what Blackburn was saying.

". . . you hadn't scared him off last night," the Oculator said, "we wouldn't *be* in this predicament."

Ms. Fletcher folded her arms. "I brought you the sands, Radrian. That's what you wanted."

Blackburn shook his head. Hands clasped behind his back, he began to stroll in a slow circle, his well-polished shoes clicking on the stones below.

"You were supposed to watch over the boy," he said, "not *just* collect the sands. This was sloppy, Shasta. Very sloppy. What possessed you to send a regular thug to go collect the child?"

Ms. Fletcher sent the gunman, I thought with a stab of anger. *She really was working for them, all this time.*

"That's what I've always done," Ms. Fletcher snapped. "I send one of my men to move the boy to another foster home."

Blackburn turned. "Your man drew a gun on a Smedry."

"That wasn't supposed to happen," Ms. Fletcher said. "Someone must have bribed him — someone from one of the other factions, I'd guess. The Order of the Shattered Lens, perhaps? We won't know for certain until the interrogation is complete, but I suspect that they were afraid that you'd manage to recruit the boy."

Recruit me? That comment made me cock my head. However, there was something more pressing in that statement. It implied that Ms. Fletcher *hadn't* wanted me killed. For some reason, that made me relieved, though I knew it was foolish.

Down below, Blackburn shook his head. "You should have gone yourself to collect him, Shasta."

"I intended to go along," Ms. Fletcher said. "But . . ."

"But what?"

She was silent for a moment. "I lost my keys," she said.

I frowned. It seemed like an odd comment to make. Blackburn, however, simply laughed at this. "It still has the better of you, doesn't it?"

I could see Ms. Fletcher flushing. "I don't see what problem you have with me. The man who tried to shoot the boy was working for someone else. We should be focusing on discovering what those sands do."

"The problem is, Shasta," Blackburn said, growing solemn again, "this operation was sloppy. When my people are sloppy, it makes *me* look incompetent. I'm not very fond of that." He paused, then looked at her. "This is not a time we can spare mistakes. Old Smedry is in this town somewhere."

Ms. Fletcher paused. "Him? You think it was *him*?"

"Who else?" Blackburn asked.

"There are a lot of elderly Oculators, Radrian," she said.

Blackburn shook his head. "I should think that you, of all people, would recognize the Old One's handiwork. He's in the city, after the same thing that we were."

"Well," Ms. Fletcher said. "If Leavenworth was here, he's gone now. He'll have the boy out of Inner Libraria before we can track him down."

"Perhaps," Blackburn said quietly.

I squirmed. As I listened, I'd revised my earlier opinion of Blackburn. I didn't like this man. Blackburn seemed too . . . thoughtful. Careful.

Dangerous.

"I've always been curious," Blackburn said, as if to himself. "Why did they leave a Smedry of the pure line to be raised in Inner Libraria? Old Leavenworth must have known that we would find the boy. That we would watch him, control him. It seems like an odd move, wouldn't you say?"

Ms. Fletcher shrugged. "Perhaps they just didn't want him. Considering his . . . parentage."

What? I thought. *Say more on that!*

But Blackburn didn't. He just shook his head thoughtfully. "Perhaps. But then this child seems to have an inordinately powerful Talent. And there were always the sands. Old Smedry must have known, as we did, that the sands would arrive on the boy's thirteenth birthday."

"So, they used the boy as bait for the sands," Ms. Fletcher said. "But we got to them first."

"And old Smedry ended up with the child. Who gained the better half of the deal, I wonder?"

Tell me where the sands are! I thought. *Say something useful!*

"As for the sands," Ms. Fletcher said. "There is the matter of payment. . . ."

Blackburn turned, and I caught a flash of emotion on his face. Anger?

Ms. Fletcher raised a finger. "You don't own me, Blackburn. Don't presume to think that you do."

"You'll get paid, woman," Blackburn said, smiling.

It was not the type of smile one wanted to see. It was dark. Dark as the footprints I had followed. Dark as the hatred in a man's eyes the moment he does something terrible to another person. Dark as an unlit street on a silent night, when you know something is out there, watching you.

It was from this smile that I realized where Radrian Blackburn got the title "Dark" Oculator.

"You would sell the child too, wouldn't you?" Blackburn said, still smiling as he removed his monocle, rubbed it clean, then placed it in his pocket. "You would pass him off for wealth, as you did with the sands. Sometimes you impress even me, Fletcher."

Ms. Fletcher shrugged.

Blackburn placed a different monocle onto his eye.

Wait, I thought. *What am I forgetting?*

And then I realized what it was. Ms. Fletcher's footprints, along with Blackburn's, shone below. I was still wearing the Tracker's Lenses. Cursing quietly, I pulled them off, then switched them for my Oculator's Lenses.

Blackburn glowed with a vibrant black cloud. He crackled with power, giving off an aura so strong that I had to blink against the terrible shining darkness.

If Blackburn gave off an aura like that . . . what did I give off?

Blackburn smiled, turning directly toward the place where I was hiding with the others. Then his monocle flashed with a burst of power.

I immediately fell unconscious.

CHAPTER 11

You probably assume you know what is going to happen next: me, tied to an altar, about to get sacrificed. Unfortunately, you're wrong. The story hasn't gotten to that part yet.

This revelation may annoy you. It may even frustrate you. If it does, then I've achieved my purpose. However, before you throw this book against the wall, you should understand something about storytelling.

Some people assume that authors write books because we have vivid imaginations and want to share our vision. Other people assume that authors write because we are bursting with stories, and therefore *must* scribble those stories down in moments of creative propondidty.

Both groups of people are completely wrong. Authors write books for one, and only one, reason: because we like to torture people.

Now, actual torture is frowned upon in civilized society. Fortunately, the authorial community has discovered in storytelling an even more powerful — and more fulfilling — means of causing agony in others. We write stories. And by doing so, we engage in a perfectly legal method of doing all kinds of mean and terrible things to our readers.

Take, for instance, the word I used above. *Propondidty.* There is no such word — I made it up. Why? Because it amused me to think of thousands of readers looking up a nonsense word in their dictionaries.

Authors also create lovable, friendly characters — then proceed to do terrible things to them (like throw them in unsightly, Librarian-controlled dungeons). This makes readers feel hurt and worried for the characters. The simple truth is that authors *like* making people squirm. If this weren't the case, all novels would be filled completely with cute bunnies having birthday parties.

So, now you know the reason why I — one of the most wealthy and famous people in the Free Kingdoms — would bother writing a book. This is the only way I can prove to all of you people that I'm not the heroic savior that you think I am. If you don't believe what I'm telling you, then ask yourself this: would any decent, kindhearted individual become a writer? Of course not.

I know how this story ends. I know what really happened to my parents. I know the true secret of the Sands of Rashid. I know how I finally ended up suspended over a bubbling pit of acidic magma, tied to a flaming altar, staring at my reflection in the twisted, cracked dagger of a Librarian executioner.

But I am not a nice person. And so, I'm not going to reveal any of these things to you. Not yet anyway.

So there.

"I can't believe how *stupid* I am!" Bastille snapped.

I blinked, slowly coming awake. I was lying on something hard.

"I should have realized Alcatraz would have an aura," Bastille continued. "It was so obvious!"

"He only just started using Oculator's Lenses, Bastille," Sing said. "You couldn't have known he'd have an aura already."

She shook her head. "I was sloppy. I just . . . have trouble thinking of that idiot as an Oculator. He doesn't seem to know anything."

I groaned and opened my eyes, discovering a bland

stone ceiling above me. The something hard I was lying on turned out to be the ground. And no, it didn't want to be friends with me.

"What happened?" I asked, rubbing my forehead.

"Shocker's Lenses," Bastille said. "Or . . . well, *one* Shocker's Lens. They cause a flash of light that knocks out anyone who's looking at the Oculator."

I grunted, sitting. "I'll have to get a set of those."

"They're *very* difficult to use," Bastille said. "I doubt you could manage it."

"Thanks for the confidence," I grumbled. We were in a cell, apparently. It felt more like a dungeon than a prison. There was a pile of straw to one side, apparently to use for sleeping, and there didn't appear to be any "facilities" besides a bucket by the wall.

It was certainly not a place I wanted to spend any extended period of time. Especially in mixed company.

I stumbled to my feet. My jacket was gone, as were Sing's bag of weapons and Bastille's handbag. "Is there anyone out there?" I asked quietly. The cell had three stone walls, while the front was set with more modern-style, cagelike bars.

"One guard," Bastille said. "Warrior."

I nodded, then took a deep breath and walked up to the front of the cell. I put one hand on the bars and activated my Talent.

Or, at least, I tried to. Nothing happened.

Bastille snorted. "It won't work, Smedry. Those bars are made from Reinforcer's Glass. Things like Smedry Talents and Oculator powers won't affect them."

"Oh," I said, lowering my hand.

"What did you expect to do anyway?" she snapped. "Save us? What about the soldier out there? What about the Dark Oculator, who is in the room next door?"

"I didn't think —"

"No. No, you Smedrys *never* think! You make all this talk about 'seeing' and 'information,' but you never do anything useful. You don't plan, you just *go*. And you drag the rest of us along with you!"

She spun and walked as far from me as she could, then sat down on the floor, not looking at me.

I stood silent, a little stupefied.

"Don't mind her, Alcatraz," Sing said quietly, joining me at the front of the cell. "She's just a little angry with herself for letting us get caught."

"It wasn't her fault," I said. "It was mine."

It was mine. Not words I'd often said. I was a little surprised to hear them come out of my mouth.

"Actually," Sing said, "it's really not *any* of our fault. You were right to suggest following Blackburn — he was probably our best chance of finding the sands. But, well, this is how things turned out."

Sing sighed, running his hand along one of the bars. I reached out and felt one too, noting now that Bastille had been right — the bar didn't quite feel like iron. It was too smooth.

"There were a few Smedrys who could have gotten through these bars, Reinforcer's Glass or no," Sing said. "Ah, to have a Talent like that . . ."

"I think your Talent is pretty useful," I said. "It saved us down below, and that stumble you did to create a distraction was great. I've never seen anything so amazing!"

Sing smiled. "I know you're just saying that. But I appreciate it anyway."

We stood quietly for a moment, and I found myself feeling frustrated, and more than a little guilty. Despite what Sing had said, I felt responsible for getting us captured. Slowly, the real weight of what was going on began to press against me.

I'd been imprisoned by the type of people who sent armed gunmen to collect young boys from their homes — people who included a man so evil, he left dark footprints burning on the ground. Blackburn obviously could have killed me if he'd wanted. That meant he had kept me alive for a reason. And I was growing more and more certain I didn't want to know what that reason was.

It had been a long time since I'd felt true dread. I'd learned over the years to be a bit callous — I'd had to, with my foster parents abandoning me so often. In that moment, however, dread pushed through my shell.

Bastille was still sulking in the back, so I glanced at Sing, looking for some sort of comfort. "Sing? Our ancestors — could you tell me about some of them?"

"What would you like to know?"

I shrugged.

"Well," Sing said, rubbing his chin. "There was Libby Smedry — she was quite the capable one. I've often wished to have a Talent half as grand as hers."

"And it was?"

"She could get impossible amounts of water on the floor when she did the dishes," Sing said, sighing slightly. "She single-handedly ended the drought in Kalbeeze during the fourth-third century — and she did it while keeping all of their dishware sparkling clean!"

He smiled wistfully. "Also, I suppose everyone knows about Alcatraz Smedry the Seventh — he would be about sixteen generations removed from you. The Librarians weren't around then, but Dark Oculators were. Alcatraz Seven had the Talent to make annoying noises at inappropriate times. He defeated enemy after enemy — you see, he distracted the Dark Oculators so much that they couldn't concentrate hard enough to work their Lenses!"

Sing sighed. "Thinking about those kinds of Talents always makes tripping seems so bland."

"Breaking things isn't all that great either," I said.

"No, Alcatraz. Breaking things — now that's a *real* Talent. One of the great old talents, talked about in the legends. I know I shouldn't really complain about my power — I should be happy to have anything. But you . . . it would be a true shame to speak ill of a Talent like that. And it couldn't have been given to a better Smedry."

A better Smedry . . .

Sing smiled at me encouragingly, and I glanced away. *I'm getting too attached to him,* I thought. *To all of them — Grandpa Smedry, Sing, even Bastille.*

"Come on," Sing said. "Don't look so glum."

"You don't really know me, Sing," I found myself saying. "I'm not a good person."

"Nonsense!" Sing said.

I leaned against the bars of the cell, glancing out — not that there was much to look at. A simple stone wall stood across from the cell. "You don't know the things I've done, Sing. The . . . breaking. The pain I've brought to good people — people who just wanted to give me a home."

Sing shrugged. "Actually, Alcatraz, Grandpa Smedry spoke of you sometimes. He talked about the . . . mishaps that happened around you. He said he thought it might be related to your Talent, and turns out it was. Not your fault at all!"

Why did you burn down your foster parents' kitchen? Grandpa Smedry had asked. *It seems like a perversion of your Talent. . . .*

"No," I said. "It *was* my fault, Sing. I didn't break simple, ordinary things. I broke the things that were the most valuable to people who cared for me. I made them hate me. On purpose."

"No," Sing said. "No, that doesn't sound like something a Smedry could do."

"Every family has its black sheep, Sing," I said. "I'm

173

a . . . broken Smedry. Maybe that's why the Dark Oculator didn't kill me. Maybe he knows that I'm not noble like the rest of you. Maybe he knows that he might be able to pull me to his side. Perhaps I'd be better there."

Sing fell silent. I waited for him to look horrified or betrayed.

After a few moments, Sing raised a hand and put it on my shoulder. "You're still my cousin. Even if you've done bad things, that doesn't make you a Dark Oculator. Anything you've done, you can fix. You can change."

It's not that easy, I thought. *Will Sing be that forgiving when I accidentally break something precious to him? His books, perhaps? What will Sing Smedry do when he finds all that he loves broken and mangled, discarded at the feet of the disaster known as Alcatraz Smedry?*

Sing smiled, removing his hand from my shoulder, apparently thinking that the problem was resolved. But it wasn't, not for me. I sat down on the stones, arms around my knees. *What's wrong with me lately? Sing seems determined to like me. Why am I so concerned with making certain he knows what I've done?*

I turned away from Sing and, for some reason, found myself thinking about days long past.

I have trouble remembering the first things I broke. They were valuable, though — I remember that. Expensive crystal things, collected by my first foster mother. It seemed that I could barely walk by her room without one of them shattering.

That wasn't all either. Any room they locked me in I could escape without even really trying. Anything they bought or brought into the home, the curious young Alcatraz would study and inspect.

And break.

So, they got rid of me. They hadn't been cruel people — I'd just been too much for them. I saw them once, on the street a few months later, walking with a little girl. My replacement. A girl who didn't break everything she touched, a girl who fit better into what they had imagined for their lives.

I shivered, sitting with my back to the glass bars of my prison cell. Sometimes I tried — I tried *so* hard — not to break anything. But it was like the Talent welled up inside of me when I did that. And then, when it burst free, it was even more powerful.

A tear rolled down my cheek. After moving from family to family enough times, I'd realized that they would all leave me eventually. After that, I hadn't worried as much about what I broke. In fact . . . I'd begun to break things more often — important things. The valuable cars of a father who collected vehicles. The trophies won by a father who had played sports in college. The kitchen of a mother who was a renowned chef.

I'd told myself that these things were simply accidents. But now I saw a pattern in my life.

I broke things early, quickly. The most valuable, important things. That way, they'd know. They'd know what I was.

And they'd send me away. Before I could come to care for them. And get hurt again.

It felt safer to act that way. But what had it done to me? In breaking so many objects, had I broken myself? I shivered again. Sitting in that cold Librarian dungeon — faced by my first (but certainly not last) failure as a leader — I finally admitted something to myself.

I don't just break, I thought. *I destroy.*

CHAPTER 12

At this point, perhaps you feel sorry for me. Or perhaps you feel that my suffering was deserved, considering what I'd done to all those families who tried to take me in.

I'd like to tell you that all of this soul-searching was good for me. And perhaps it did help in the short term. However, before you get your hopes up, let me promise you here and now that the Alcatraz Smedry you think you know is a farce. You may see some promising things developing in my young self, but in the end, none of these things were able to save those I love.

If I could go back, I'd drive Sing and the others away for good. Unfortunately, at that point in my life, I still had some small hope that I'd find acceptance with them. I should have realized that attachment would only lead to pain. Especially when I failed to protect them.

Still, it was probably good for me to realize that I was driving people away on purpose, for it let me understand just how bad a person I am. Perhaps more young boys should be captured by evil Librarians, forced to sit in cold dungeons, contemplating their faults as they wait for their doom. Perhaps I'll start a summer camp based on that theme.

The weirdest part about this all, I thought, *is that nobody yet has made a joke about a pair of kids named Alcatraz and Bastille getting locked in a prison.*

Of course, we weren't in a very jokey mood at that moment. I couldn't know for certain, since the hourglass — along with my jacket — had been taken from me, but I figured that our remaining half hour had passed, and then some. I tried very hard not to look at the latrine bucket, in the hopes that it wouldn't remind my body of any duties that needed to be done.

Yet as I sat and thought, some very strange things were happening to me. I'd always kind of thought of myself as a defiant rebel against the system. However, the truth was that I was just a whiny kid who threw tantrums and broke things because he wanted to make certain that he hurt others before they hurt him. It was that dreaded humility again, and it was having a very odd effect on me. It should have made me feel like a worm, crushing me down with shame. Yet for some reason, it didn't do that.

Realizing my faults didn't make my head bow but made me look up instead. Realizing how stupid I had been didn't cause me grief but made me smile at my own foolishness. Losing my identity didn't make me feel paranoid or worthless.

The truth was, I'd secretly felt all of those things — shame, grief, paranoia, insecurity — for most of my life. Now that I wasn't covering them up, I could begin to let go of them. It didn't make me a perfect person, and it didn't change what I'd done. However, it did let me stand up and face my situation with a little more determination.

I was a Smedry. And while I wasn't quite certain of all that meant, I was beginning to have a better idea. I crossed the room, passing Sing, and crouched down by Bastille.

"Bastille," I whispered. "We've waited long enough. We have to figure a way to get out of here."

She glanced up at me, and I could see that her face was streaked with tears. I blinked in surprise. *Why has* she *been crying?*

"Get out?" she said. "We can't get out! This cell was *built* to hold people like you and me."

"There has to be a way."

"I've failed," Bastille said quietly, as if she hadn't heard me.

"*Bastille*," I said. "We don't have time for this."

"What do you know?" she snapped. "You've been an Oculator all of your life, and have you done anything with it? Never! You didn't even know. How is that fair?"

I paused, then reached up to touch my face. I hadn't even noticed — my glasses were gone.

Of course they are, I thought. *They took my jacket with the Tracker's Lenses and the Firebringer's Lenses in the pocket. They took Bastille's and Sing's Warrior's Lenses. They would have taken my Oculator's Lenses.*

"You didn't even notice, did you?" Bastille asked bitterly. "They took your most powerful possession, and you didn't even notice."

"I haven't been wearing them for long," I said. "Only a few hours, really. I guess it felt natural to me for them to *not* be there when I woke up."

"Natural for them to not be there," Bastille said, shaking

her head. "Why do *you* get to be an Oculator, Smedry? Why you?"

"Aren't all Smedrys Oculators?" I asked. "Or, at least, all of those in the pure line?"

"Most of them are," she said. "But not all of them. And there are plenty of Oculators who *aren't* Smedrys."

"Obviously," I said, glancing over my shoulder, toward the room where Blackburn and Ms. Fletcher supposedly were.

Then I glanced back at Bastille, cocking my head. She stared at me defiantly. *That's it. That's what I've been missing.* "You wanted to be one, didn't you?" I asked. "An Oculator."

"It's none of your business, Smedry."

But it made too much sense to ignore. "That's why you know so much about Oculator auras. And you were the one who identified the Lenses that Blackburn used on us. You must have studied a whole lot to learn so many things."

"For all the good it did," she said with a quiet snort. "I learned that studying can't change a person, Smedry. I've always wanted to be something I wasn't — and the thing is, everyone supported me. 'You can be anything you want, if you try hard enough!' they said.

"Well, you know what, Smedry? They lied. There are some things that you just *can't* change."

I stood silently.

Bastille shook her head. "You can't study yourself into being something you aren't. I won't ever be an Oculator. I'll have to settle for being what my mother always told me I *should* be. The thing I'm apparently 'gifted' in."

"And that is?" I asked.

"Being a warrior," she said with a sigh. "But I guess I'm not too good at that either."

Now, you're probably expecting poor Bastille to "learn something" by the end of this book. You probably expect to see her overcome her bitterness, to realize that she never should have given up on her dreams.

You think this because you've read too many silly stories about people who achieve things they previously thought impossible — deep and poignant books about trains that climb hills or little girls who succeed through sheer determination.

Let me make one thing very clear. Bastille will *never* become an Oculator. It's a genetic ability, which means you can only become an Oculator if your ancestors were Oculators. Bastille's weren't.

People can do great things. However, there are some things they just *can't* do. I, for instance, have not been able to transform myself into a Popsicle, despite years of effort. I could, however, make myself insane, if I wished. (Though if I achieved the second, I might be able to make myself *think* I'd achieved the first. . . .)

Anyway, if there's a lesson to be learned, it's this: Great success often depends upon being able to distinguish between the impossible and the improbable. Or, in easier terms, distinguishing between Popsicles and insanity.

Any questions?

I wanted to say something to help Bastille. After all, I'd just undergone a life-changing revelation, and I figured that there should be enough to go around. Unfortunately, Bastille wasn't exactly in a "life-changing revelation" sort of mood.

"I don't need your pity, Smedry," she snapped, swatting my arm away. "I'm just fine as I am. There really isn't anything you could do to help anyway."

I opened my mouth to reply, but at that moment, I heard a door open. I turned as Ms. Fletcher strolled into the hallway outside our cell.

"Hello, Smedry," she said.

"Ms. Fletcher," I said flatly. "Or 'Shasta,' or whatever your real name is."

"Fletcher will do," she said, obviously trying to sound friendly. She couldn't quite pull it off. "I've come to chat."

I shook my head. "I have little to say to you."

"Come now, Alcatraz. I've always looked out for you, despite how difficult you made my life. Surely you can see that I have your best interests at heart."

"Somehow I doubt that, Ms. Fletcher."

She raised an eyebrow. "That's all you have to say? I expected something a little more . . . scathing, Smedry."

"Actually, I've changed," I said. "You see, I just had a life-changing revelation and don't plan to make snide comments anymore."

"Is that so?"

"Yes, it is," I said firmly.

Ms. Fletcher cocked her head, a strange look on her face. "What?" I asked.

"Nothing," she said. "You just . . . reminded me of someone I used to know. Anyway, I don't care what game you are playing today. The time has come for us to deal."

"Deal?"

Ms. Fletcher nodded, leaning in. "We want the old man. The crazy one who came and got you this morning."

"You mean Grandpa Smedry?" I asked, glancing at Sing, who was watching quietly. Apparently, he was content to let me take the lead in the conversation.

"Yes," Ms. Fletcher said. "Grandpa Smedry. Tell us where he is, and we'll let you go."

"Let me go? Let me go where?"

"Out," Ms. Fletcher said, motioning with her hand. "We'll find you another foster family, and things can go back to the way they were."

"That hardly seems compelling," I said.

"Alcatraz," Ms. Fletcher said flatly. "You're in a Librarian dungeon, and you have Oculator blood. If you aren't careful, you'll end up as a sacrifice. I'd be a little more friendly if I were you — I'm likely the only ally you'll find in this place."

This was, of course, the first time I ever heard about a ceremony involving sacrificial Oculators. I dismissed the comment as an idle threat.

Foolish, foolish Alcatraz.

"If you're the best ally I have, Ms. Fletcher," I said, "then I'm in serious trouble."

"That sounded just a little bit snide, Alcatraz," Sing said helpfully. "You may want to back off a little."

"Thank you, Sing," I said, still watching Ms. Fletcher, my eyes narrowed.

"I can get you out, Alcatraz," Ms. Fletcher said. "Don't make me do something we'd both regret. I've watched over you for years, haven't I? You can trust me."

Watched over you for years . . . "Yes," I said. "Yes, you *have* watched over me. And every time a family abandoned me, you told me I was useless. It was like you *wanted* me to feel abandoned and unimportant." I met her eyes. "That's it, isn't it? You were worried I'd come to understand and control my power — you worried that I'd learn what it meant to be a Smedry. That's why you always treated me like you did. You needed me to be insecure, so that I would trust you — and distrust my Talent."

Ms. Fletcher looked away. "Look, let's just make a deal. Let me get you out, and we can forget about the past for now."

"And these others?" I asked, nodding toward Sing and Bastille. "If I go free, what happens to them?"

"What do you care?" Ms. Fletcher asked, looking back at me.

I folded my arms.

"You *have* changed," Ms. Fletcher said. "And not for the better, I'd say. Is this the same boy who burned down a kitchen yesterday? Since when did you start caring about the people around you?"

The answer to that question was actually "About five minutes ago." However, I didn't intend to share that information with Ms. Fletcher.

"Okay," I said. "We'll have an exchange. You want to know where the old man is? Well, I want to know some things too. Answer my questions, and I'll answer yours."

"Fine," Ms. Fletcher said, folding her arms.

Businesslike as always, I thought. "How did you know about the Sands of Rashid?"

Ms. Fletcher waved an indifferent hand. "Your parents promised them to you at your birth. It's a custom — to pronounce an inheritance upon a newborn and deliver it on the child's thirteenth birthday. Everyone knew that you were *supposed* to get those sands. Some of us are a little surprised that they actually made their way to you, but we were happy to see them nonetheless."

"Did you know my parents, then?"

"Of course," Ms. Fletcher said. "Actually, I studied under

them. I thought they might be able to train me to be an Oculator."

I snorted. "That's not something you can learn."

"Yes, well," Ms. Fletcher said, looking a little flustered, "I was young."

"Were you friends with them, then?" I asked.

"I got along better with your father than your mother," Ms. Fletcher said.

"Did you kill them?" I asked, teeth gritted.

Ms. Fletcher laughed a flat, lifeless laugh. "Of course not. Do I look like a killer?"

"You sent a man with a gun after me."

"That was a mistake," Ms. Fletcher said. "Besides, your parents were Smedrys. They would be even harder to kill than you."

"And why do you want Grandpa Smedry?" I asked.

"No, I think I've answered enough questions," Ms. Fletcher said. "Now, fulfill your end of the bargain. Where is the old man?"

I smiled. "I forgot."

"But . . . our bargain!"

"I lied, Ms. Fletcher," I said. "I do that sometimes."

See, I promised you. Life-changing revelation or not, I never was all that good a person.

Ms. Fletcher's eyes opened wide, and she displayed more emotion than I'd ever seen from her as she began muttering at me under her breath.

"Enough!" a new voice said. A dark-suited arm shoved Ms. Fletcher away, and Blackburn moved over to stand in front of the cell.

"Tell me where the old fool is, boy," Blackburn said quietly. He stared at me, his monocle glistening with a reddish color. Even without my Oculator's Lenses, I swear that I could see a little black cloud rising from him.

"If you don't talk willingly," Blackburn said, reaching up to take off his monocle, "I will *make* you." He pulled another monocle from a vest pocket. It had green and black tints. "This is a Torturer's Lens. By looking through it and focusing on a part of your body, I can make you feel intense agony. It makes the muscles begin to rip, and while it *probably* won't kill you, you will soon start to wish that it would."

He reached up, putting the monocle in place. "I've seen men permanently paralyzed by these things, boy. I've seen them break their own bones as they thrash about on the ground, crying out with such pain that they'd have killed themselves to stop it. Does that sound like fun? Well, if not, you should start talking. *Now!*"

It's funny what a little taste of leadership can do to someone. A shade of responsibility, a smidgen of self-understanding, and I was ready to stand up to a full-blooded Dark Oculator. I gritted my teeth, jutted out my chin defiantly, and stared him in the eye.

So, of course, I got my heroic little self blasted with a beam of pure pain.

This is supposed to be a book for all ages, so I won't go into details about how it felt to get hit by a Torturer's Lens. Just try and remember the worst wound you've ever felt. The most agonizing, most terrifying pain in your life. Remember it, hold it in your head.

Then imagine if a shark swam by and bit you in half while you were distracted. That's a little what it felt like. Only, add in swallowing a few grenades and suffering through a night at the opera too. (And don't *try* and tell me I didn't warn you about the sharks.)

The pain let up. I lay on the floor of the cell, though I didn't remember falling. Sing was at my side, and even Bastille was moving over to me, her face concerned. My agony faded slowly, and I looked up, seeing Blackburn as a dark shadow standing before the cell.

There was a small twist of pleasure on his lips. "Now, boy, tell me what I want to know."

And I would have. This is your hero, Free Kingdomers. I broke that easily — I hadn't ever known pain; I was no soldier. I was just a kid trapped by forces he had no hope of understanding. I would have told Blackburn anything he wanted to know.

However, I didn't have a chance to spit it out. At that moment, you see, Grandpa Smedry poked his head into the dungeon hallway, smiling happily.

"Why, hello, Blackburn," he said. Then he waved to me, holding up a pair of hands that were manacled together. He wasn't wearing his Oculator's Lenses, and a pair of beefy-looking men in dark robes and black sunglasses stood behind him, holding his arms.

"It appears that I've been captured," Grandpa Smedry said, manacle chains clinking. "I hope I'm not too late!"

CHAPTER 13

We have now spent two complete chapters trapped in the dungeon. We're about to embark on our third chapter in there, assuming I ever finish with this introduction.

Three chapters is an awfully long time in book terms. You see, time moves differently in novels. The author could, for instance, say, "And I spent fourteen years in prison, where I obtained the learning of a gentleman and discovered the location of a buried treasure." Now, this sounds like it would be a great deal of time — fourteen *years* — but it actually only took one sentence to explain. So, therefore, it happened very quickly.

Three chapters, on the other hand, is a very long time. It is a longer time than I spent in my foster home. It is a longer time than I spent visiting the gas station. It's even a longer time than I spent in childhood, which was covered in only about two sentences.

Why so long in prison? At that moment, I was struggling with the same question. Few things are more maddening than forced inactivity, and I had been forced into inactivity for two entire chapters. True, I'd made some good, deep, personal revelations — however, the time for those had passed. I would almost *rather* have been tied to an altar and sacrificed, as opposed to being forced to sit around and wait while my grandfather was towed off to be tortured.

For, you see, that was what happened in between chapters — a space of time so short that it's practically non-existent. During that void of nothingness, Blackburn laughed evilly a couple of times, then pulled Grandpa Smedry off to the "Interrogation Room." Apparently, the Dark Oculator was overjoyed at the prospect of having a fully trained Smedry to torture.

But then again, who wouldn't be?

"Come back here!" Bastille screamed, pounding the latrine bucket repeatedly against the bars. I was now even more glad that I hadn't ended up needing to use it.

"Come back and fight me!" she yelled, slamming the

bucket against the bars in one final overhand strike, venting her fury by smashing the wooden container into a dozen different pieces. She stood, puffing for a second, holding a broken handle.

"Well," Sing whispered, "at least she's getting back some of her good humor."

Right, I thought. By then, my agony had faded almost to nothingness. (I later learned that I'd only been subjected to the Torturer's Lens for a period of three seconds. It takes at least five to do permanent damage.)

I empathized with Bastille — I even felt some of her same rage, even if I didn't express it by destroying innocent bucketry. The longer I sat, the more ashamed I felt at how quickly I'd broken. Yet remembering those three seconds of pain made me shudder.

And even worse than the memory was the knowledge that my grandfather — a man I barely knew, but one for whom I already felt a sincere affection — had been captured. At that very moment, the old man was probably being subjected to the Torturer's Lens. And *his* torture would last far longer than three seconds.

Bastille reached down, picking up a few bucket shards and tossing them in annoyance at the wall outside the cell.

"That isn't helping, Bastille," I said.

"Oh?" she snapped. "And what about sitting on the ground, looking stupid? How much good is *that* doing?"

I blinked, flushing.

"Bastille, lass," Sing said quietly. "That was harsh, even for you."

Bastille puffed quietly for a few more moments, then turned away. "Whatever," she muttered, walking over to kick at the hay pile with a frustrated motion. "It's just that . . . Old Smedry . . . I mean, he's a fool, but I think of him being tortured . . ."

She kicked at the hay again, tossing a pile into the air. The way it bounced off the wall and fell back on her might have been comical, had the situation been different.

"We all care for him, Bastille," Sing said.

"You don't understand," Bastille said, picking a few strands of hay out of her silvery hair. "I'm a Knight of Crystallia! I'm sworn to protect the Oculators of the Free Kingdoms. And I was assigned to be *his* guard. I'm supposed to protect the old Smedry — keep him out of situations like this!"

"Yes, but —"

"No, Sing," Bastille said. "You really don't understand.

Leavenworth is a fully trained Smedry of the pure line. Not just that, he's a member of the Oculator Council and is the trusted friend of *dozens* of kings and rulers. Do you have any idea the kinds of state secrets he knows?"

Sing frowned, and I looked up.

"Why do you think the Council insists that he *always* keep a Knight of Crystallia around to protect him?" Bastille asked. "He complains — says he doesn't need a Crystin guard. Well, the Council would have conceded to him long ago, if it were just his life that he endangered. But he knows things, Sing. *Important* things. That's why I'm supposed to keep him out of trouble, why I'm supposed to do my best to protect him." She sighed, slumping down beside the wall. "And I failed."

And at that moment, I probably said the dumbest thing I ever have.

"Why you?" I asked. "I mean, if he's so important, why — of all people — did they choose *you* to protect him?"

Yes, it was very insensitive. No, it wasn't very helpful. However, it's what slipped out.

You know you were thinking the same thing anyway.

Bastille's eyes widened with anger, but she didn't snap at

me. Finally, she just let her head slump against her knees. "I don't know," she whispered. "They never told me — they never even explained. I had barely achieved knighthood, but they sent me anyway."

We all fell quiet.

Finally, I stood. I walked to the bars of the cell. Then I knelt. *I've broken cars, kitchens, and chickens,* I thought. *I've destroyed the homes and possessions of people who took me in. I've broken the hearts of people who wanted to love me.*

I can break the cell that is keeping me a prisoner.

I reached out, gripping the bars, then closed my eyes and focused.

Break! I commanded. Waves of power washed down my arms, tingling like jolts of electricity. They slammed into the bars.

And nothing happened.

I opened my eyes, gritting my teeth in frustration. The bars remained where they were, looking annoyingly unbroken. There wasn't even a crack in them. The lock was made of glass as well, and somehow I knew that it would react the same way to my Talent.

Again, I feel the need to point out the Popsicle lesson.

Desire does not instantly change the world. Sometimes, stories gloss over this fact, for the world would be a much more pleasant place if you could obtain something simply by wanting it badly enough.

Unfortunately, this is a real and true story, not a fantasy. I couldn't escape from the prison simply because I wanted to.

Yet I would like to note something else at this point. Determination — true determination — is more than simply *wanting* something to happen. It's wanting something to happen, then finding a realistic way to make certain that what you want to happen, happens.

And that happened to be what was happening with the story's current happenings.

I ignored the bars, instead laying my palm flat against the stones of the cell floor. They were large, sturdy blocks, plastered together with a smooth mortar. The bars ran directly into holes in the stone.

I smiled, then closed my eyes again, focusing. I hadn't often used my Talent so intentionally, but I felt that I was gaining some skill with it. I was able to send a wave of power through my arms and into the rocks.

The mortar cracked quietly beneath my fingers. I focused harder, sending out an even larger wave of breaking power.

There was a loud *crack*. When I opened my eyes, I found that I was kneeling in dust and chips, the stones beneath my knees reduced entirely to rubble.

I stared, a little shocked at just how much of the stone I had broken. Sing stood, looking on with a surprised expression. Even Bastille looked up from her mourning. Cracks in the stone twisted across the floor, spiderwebbing all the way to the back of the cell.

They keep saying that my Talent is powerful, I thought. *How much could I really break, if I set my mind to it?* Eagerly, I reached up, grabbing a bar and trying to pull it free from its now-rubbled mountings.

It remained firm. It didn't even budge a bit.

"Did you really think that would work?" an amused voice asked.

I looked up at the dungeon guard, who had walked over to watch me. He wore the clothing one might have expected of a Librarian — an unfashionable knit vest pulled tight over a buttoned pink shirt, matched by a slightly darker pink bow tie. His glasses even had a bit of tape on them.

Only one thing about him deviated from what I would have expected: He was huge. He was as tall as Sing, and easily twice as muscular. It was like a bodybuilder supersoldier had beaten up an unfortunate nerd and — for some inconceivable reason — stolen his clothing.

The guard punched a fist into his palm, smiling. He wore a sword tied at his waist, and his glasses — the taped ones — were dark, like the ones that Sing and Bastille wore. Once again, I was struck by the unfairness of letting the warriors wear sunglasses, while I was stuck with slightly pink ones.

That is one complaint, by the way, I still haven't gotten over.

"The stones are just there for show," the Librarian said. "The entire cage is made from Reinforcer's Glass — it's a box, with the bars at the front. Breaking the stones won't do any good. You think we aren't familiar with Smedry tricks?"

He's too far away to touch, I thought with frustration. *But . . . what was it Grandpa Smedry said when I destroyed that gunman's weapon?*

That man had threatened me. And my Talent had worked proactively, instinctively.

At a distance.

I reached down, picking up a few pieces of wood from

the broken bucket. The beefy Librarian snorted and turned to walk back to his post. I, however, tossed a piece of wood through the bars, hitting him in the back of the head.

The guard turned, frowning. I bounced another piece of wood off of his forehead.

"Hey!" the Librarian snapped.

I threw harder, this time causing the Librarian to flinch as the bit of wood came close to his eyes.

"Alcatraz?" Sing asked nervously. "Are you certain this is wise?" Bastille, however, stood up. She walked toward the front of the cell.

I threw again.

"Stop that!" the Librarian said, stepping forward, raising his fists.

I threw a fifth piece of wood, hitting him in the chest.

"All right," the Librarian said, reaching down to unsheathe his sword. "What do you think of this?" He stuck the sword forward, apparently intending to force me back with it.

Bastille, however, moved more quickly. I watched with shock as she grabbed the blade of the sword, somehow managing to keep from cutting herself as she yanked it forward.

This threw the Librarian off balance, and he stumbled toward the cell, still holding on to his weapon.

Bastille snapped forward, reaching between the bars and grabbing the Librarian guard by the hair. Then she yanked the man's head down and forward, slamming it against the glass bars.

The sword clanged to the ground. The guard's unconscious body followed a second later. Bastille knelt down, grabbing the guard's arm and pulling him up against the cell bars. Then she began fishing around in his pockets. "All right, Smedry," she admitted, "that was well done."

"Uh, no problem," I said. "You . . . took him down pretty smoothly."

Bastille shrugged, pulling something out of the man's pocket — a glass sphere. "He's just a Librarian thug."

"No match for a trained Knight of Crystallia," Sing agreed. "Yes, that was indeed quite clever, Alcatraz. How did you know he'd lose his temper and pull out the sword?"

"Actually," I said, "I was trying to get him to throw something at me."

Bastille frowned. "What good would that do?"

"I figured it would engage my Talent if he tried to hurt me."

Sing rubbed his chin. "That would probably have broken the thing he threw at you. But . . . how was that going to get us out of the cell?"

I paused. "I hadn't exactly gotten that far yet."

Bastille placed the glass sphere against the lock. It clicked; the door swung open.

"Either way," she said, "we're out." She glanced at me, and I could see something in her eyes. Relief, even a bit of gratitude. It wasn't an apology — but from Bastille, it was virtually the same thing. I took it for what it was worth.

Bastille left the cell and stooped down beside the unconscious Librarian. She pulled off his sunglasses, removed the tape — which was apparently there just for show — then slipped the glasses on her own face. After that, she grabbed the guard by one arm and pulled him into the cell. She quickly patted him down, pulling out a wallet and a dagger as Sing and I left the cell. Then she closed the door, using the glass sphere to lock it again.

She grinned and held up the sphere to me. "Would you mind?"

I smiled as well, then reached out with one finger and touched the sphere. It shattered.

She dug in the wallet for a moment. "Nothing useful

in here," she noted. "Except maybe this." She pulled out a small card.

"A library card?" I asked.

"What else?" she said. I took it from her fingers, turning it over.

"Hey, they're gone," Sing said. He was peeking into the room beside the dungeon, the one where Grandpa Smedry, Ms. Fletcher, and the Dark Oculator had gone.

Bastille and I joined him. The room was indeed empty, except for our possessions, which had been carefully set out on a table.

"Thank the First Sands," Bastille said with relief, tossing aside the guard's sword in favor of her handbag. "I was worried that I'd be stuck with those common weapons. I'd almost rather have had some guns."

"Now, that's not very nice," Sing said, waddling forward to inspect his guns, which sat on the table beside the gym bag.

I joined the two of them at the table as Bastille replaced her silver jacket. "There, Smedry," she said. My three pairs of glasses sat on the table. I grabbed the Oculator's Lenses eagerly, slipping them on.

Of course, nothing really *changed*. And yet, it did. Even though I wasn't used to wearing glasses, I found myself comforted to feel their weight on my face. I grabbed the other two pairs, the Firebringer's Lenses still inside their small pouch.

"We have to move quickly," Bastille said.

Sing nodded, checking the clip on a handgun. He tucked several uzis into the front of his kimono belt, threw on four separate handgun holsters, then strapped the shotgun onto his back. He soon looked like some bizarre fat Rambo samurai.

"We have to find the room where they took your grandfather," Bastille said.

"No problem," I said, slipping off my Oculator's Lenses, then putting on the Tracker's Lenses. Though Blackburn's footprints had disappeared, Grandpa Smedry's prints blazed a fiery white, still present. They led out the door on the far side of the room. Ms. Fletcher's diverged from them, heading in a different direction.

We'll have to worry about her later, I thought, nodding toward the other two. Sing slung the gym bag over his shoulder — it was still filled with ammunition — and we set off, moving quickly out after Grandpa Smedry's footprints.

And so, I managed to escape from my first dungeon. Determination can actually take you quite far — though, admittedly, you sometimes have to rely on the thirteen-year-old girl to knock out the guards.

CHAPTER 14

Yes, you're very clever. You noticed a problem.

In the last chapter, Sing, Bastille, and I escaped from prison, then immediately rushed off to save Grandpa Smedry. But, of course, Grandpa Smedry was being tortured by the very same man who had captured Sing and Bastille and me in the first place.

That meant we were in vaguely the same position as before. How did we intend to defeat a master Oculator — a dark, powerful man with more experience than all of us combined? Well, the answer is simple.

While imprisoned, we had gained a newfound wisdom. We came to a greater understanding of the world around us and of our place in it. We gained insight regarding our . . .

Oh, all right. None of us paused to think about what we

were doing. In our defense, we were a little bit flustered at the time. Plus, two of us were Smedrys.

That ought to explain it.

"This way," I said, pointing down another castlelike corridor, following Grandpa Smedry's footprints. And as we ran, something occurred to me. (No, not the fact that we were running after the man who had so easily captured us previously. Something else.)

"These corridors look familiar," I said.

"That's because *all* the corridors in this place look the same," Bastille said.

"No," I said. "It's not just that. That lantern bracket looks like a cantaloupe."

"They're all designed to look like one fruit or another," Bastille said.

"And we've passed this one before," I said.

"You think we're going in circles?" Bastille asked.

"No," I said. "I think we passed it while chasing down Blackburn that first time. That's the lantern I saw that made me ask you about electric lights. That means —"

Sing tripped.

I stood for just a brief moment. Then I dove for the

ground. Sing didn't even try to keep his balance, and he toppled like a felled tree. Bastille also threw herself down with a vengeance, as if determined to get to the floor first. All three of us hit, dropping as fast as a group of pathological martyrs at a grenade testing ground.

Nothing happened.

"Well?" I asked, glancing around.

"I don't see anything," Bastille whispered. "Sing?"

"I think I bruised something," he muttered, rubbing his side. "One of these pistols jammed me in the tummy!"

I snorted quietly. "Be glad it didn't go off. Now, why did you trip?"

"Because my foot hit something," Sing said. "That's usually how it works, Alcatraz."

"But there was nothing in this hallway to trip on!" I said. "The floor is perfectly level."

Sing nodded. "You have to have a real Talent to trip like I do."

"Which returns us to my original question," I said. "Is there a reason why we all had to hit the deck like that? This floor isn't very comfortable."

"Floors rarely are," Sing said.

"Hush!" Bastille said, scanning the corridor. "I thought I heard something."

We fell silent for a moment. Finally, Sing shrugged. "Sometimes a trip is just a trip, I guess. Maybe I —"

The wall exploded.

It *really* exploded. Rubble flew across the corridor, bits of shattered rock spraying against the wall just above me. I cried out, covering my head with my arms as chips and pebbles showered down.

The explosion opened up a large section in the wall to my left. I could see through the opening to where a hulking shadow stood in the clearing dust.

"An Alivened!" Bastille yelled, scrambling up.

I stood, bits of broken stone tumbling off my clothing. The creature obviously wasn't human. It was misshapen — its arms were far too wide and long, and they jutted out of the body in a threatening posture. In a way, the upper half of its body looked like an enormous "M," though I had rarely seen a letter of the alphabet look quite so dangerous.

As the dust settled, I could see that the thing was pale white, with patterns of gray and black peppering its wrinkled skin. In fact, it looked like . . .

"Paper?" I asked. "That thing is made of wadded-up pieces of paper?"

Bastille cursed, then grabbed me by the shoulder and shoved me down the corridor. "Run!" she said.

The urgency in her voice made me obey, and I took off. Sing ran behind, and Bastille backed away from the broken wall, looking on warily as the lumbering paper monster pulled its way through the hole and into the corridor.

"Bastille!" I yelled.

"Come on, lad!" Sing said from beside me. "Regular Aliveneds are bad enough — but a Codexian . . . well, they're the most powerful of the lot."

"But Bastille!"

"She'll follow, lad. She's just giving us a head start!"

I let myself get pulled along. However, I watched over my shoulder as I ran, keeping an eye on Bastille. She ducked a few swings from the massive creature. Then finally, she turned and began to run.

Fast.

You Hushlanders likely have never seen a Knight of Crystallia use her abilities to her fullest potential. People like Bastille spend years practicing inside of their city kingdom, training their bodies, bonding to their swords, learning to use Warrior's Lenses, and finally being implanted with a certain magical crystal. (Though, again, the Free Kingdomers consider this to be technology, rather than magic.) Only the best trainees are given the title of knight. To this day, Bastille holds the record for attaining the rank at the youngest age.

Regardless, all of this training and special preparation means that when Crystins want to run, they can really *run*. I was shocked as I saw Bastille take off after us, dashing with a speed that would have made any Olympic sprinter give up and become an accountant.

Sing yelled suddenly, lurching to a halt. I, unfortunately, was following right behind him and, as I turned, I was met by a chestful of Mokian posterior. Sing wasn't a Crystin, but he was wearing Warrior's Lenses, which probably helped him keep his balance as I bounced off of him and fell back into the hallway.

"Sing?" I said. "What —"

The large anthropologist reached to his waist, pulling out a pair of handguns. And then — with the flair of a man who had watched too many action movies — he began to unload them at something farther down the corridor. I twisted to the side and was met by the sight of another Alivened — also made completely from wadded-up pieces of paper — lumbering down the hallway in front of us.

Sing's guns had little effect on the creature. Bits of paper flipped into the air as the bullets tore through the Alivened's body. Each impact seemed to slow it a bit, but it still continued to move toward Sing at an unsteady pace.

Bastille pulled up beside me. "Shattered Glass!" she cursed, turning. The Alivened behind us was quickly approaching. "You'd better do something, Smedry," she said, whipping her handbag off her shoulder. "I don't know if I can handle these things on my own."

With that, she reached into the purse and grabbed something inside. She whipped her hand out, throwing the bag aside as she drew forth a massive crystalline sword.

I blinked. Yes, the thing Bastille had pulled from her purse was, indeed, a sword. It was nearly as tall as Bastille was, and it glittered in the lantern light, refracting a spray of rainbow colors across the corridor.

The handbag, of course, couldn't have held something so long. However, if the pulling of a sword from a handbag is the thing in this story that stops you, then you likely need therapy. I could recommend a good psychologist. Of course, he's Librarian controlled. They all are.

It's a union thing.

Bastille jumped forward, her sword glistening as she charged the Alivened. It swung at her, and she rolled, just barely ducking beneath its massive arm. Then she sliced, shearing the thing's arm completely free.

The arm fell off, its wrinkled pages suddenly straightening and bursting into the air — like those of a book that had suddenly had its binding torn free. They fluttered as they fell. The Alivened, however, didn't seem to mind the missing limb — and I soon saw why. The lumps of paper in its body surged forward, forming a new arm to replace the one that Bastille had cut free.

I finally shook myself from my daze, scrambling to my feet. Behind me, Sing pulled out twin uzis. He knelt, holding the weapons with meaty hands, and automatic weapon fire echoed in the corridor. His Alivened paused from the shock, a flurry of paper scraps exploding from its body. It stumbled for a moment, then continued on despite the rain of bullets.

"Alcatraz!" Sing yelled over the gunfire. "Do something!"

I ran to the side of the corridor, grabbing a lantern off

the wall. The cantaloupe-shaped holder broke free easily beneath my Talent, and I turned, hurling it at Sing's Alivened as Sing ran out of bullets.

The lantern crashed into the Alivened, then bounced free. The creature did not catch on fire.

"Not like that!" Sing said, reloading his uzis. "Nobody would build an Alivened out of paper without also making it resistant to a little fire!"

Sing raised the uzis and fired another spray of bullets. The thing slowed but pressed on, continuing its inevitable march.

Now, if you are ever writing a story such as this, you should know something. Never interrupt the flow of a good action scene by interjecting needless explanations. I did this once, in Chapter Fourteen of an otherwise very exciting story. I regret it to this day.

Also, if you are ever attacked by unstoppable monsters created entirely from bad romance novels, you should do exactly what I did: Quickly reach into your pocket and pull free your Firebringer's Lenses.

Resistant to a little fire, eh? I thought, yanking open the velvet pouch. *What about a* lot *of fire?!*

I reached into the pouch with desperate fingers, whipping out the Lenses — yet, as before, my touch was too unpracticed, and I was too powerful for my own good. The Lenses activated as soon as I touched them.

They began to glow dangerously.

"Gak!" I said. I tried to get the Lenses turned around. However, I fumbled, spinning the Lenses so they pointed backward at me instead.

At that moment, my Talent proactively broke the spectacles' frames. Both Lenses fell to the ground, one shattering as it hit the stones, the other bouncing away and falling facedown. It fired, blasting a stream of concentrated light into the stones beneath it.

"Alcatraz!" Sing said desperately as his uzis ran out of bullets again. He dropped them, reaching over his shoulder to pull out the shotgun. He fired it with a loud boom. The Alivened's chest exploded with a burst of paper, spraying confetti across the corridor.

The creature stumbled, nearly falling as Sing hit it again. However, it righted itself and continued to walk toward him.

I reached for the intact Firebringer's Lens, but shied back

from the heat. The Lens itself wasn't hot, of course — that would make it fairly difficult to wear on the face. However, it was superheating the stones around it, and I couldn't get close.

I turned urgently to check on Bastille, and I was just in time to see her ram her crystal sword directly into her opponent's chest. The Alivened, however, slammed its bulky arm into her, tossing her backward. The sword remained jutting ineffectively from its chest, and Bastille crashed into the stone wall of the corridor, crumpling.

"Bastille!" I shouted.

She did not move. The creature loomed over her.

Now, as I've tried to explain, I wasn't a particularly brave boy. But it has been my experience that doing something brave is much like saying something stupid.

You rarely plan on it happening.

I charged the Alivened monster. It turned toward me, stepping away from Bastille, and raised its arm to swing. I somehow managed to duck the blow. Stumbling, I reached up and grabbed the sword in the creature's chest. I pulled it free.

Or, rather, I pulled the hilt free.

I stumbled back, raising the hilt to swing before I

realized that the crystal blade was still sticking in the monster's chest.

Behind me, Sing's shotgun began to click, out of ammunition.

I lowered my hand, staring at the hilt. My Talent, unpredictable as always, had broken the sword. I stood for a long moment — far longer, undoubtedly, than I should have in those circumstances. I gripped the broken hilt.

And began to grow angry.

All my life, my Talent had ruled me. I'd pretended to go along with it, pretended that I was the one in control, but that had been a sham. I'd purposely driven my foster families away because I'd known that sooner or later, the Talent would do it for me — no matter what I wanted.

It was my master. It defined who I was. I couldn't be myself — whoever that was — because I was too busy getting into trouble for breaking things.

Grandpa Smedry and the others called my Talent a blessing. Yet I had trouble seeing that. Even during the infiltration, it seemed like the Talent had been only accidentally useful. Power was nothing without control.

The Alivened stepped forward, and I looked up, teeth clenched in frustration. I gripped the sword hilt tightly.

I don't want this, I thought. *I never wanted any of this! Bastille wanted to be an Oculator . . . well, I just wanted one thing.*

To be normal!

The hilt began to break in my hand, the carefully welded bits of steel falling free and clinking to the ground. "You want breaking?" I yelled at the Alivened. "You want *destruction?*"

The creature swung at me, and I screamed, slamming my hand palm-forward to the floor. A surge of Talent electrified my body, focusing through my chest and then down my arm. It was a jolt of power like I'd never summoned before.

The floor broke. Or perhaps *shattered* would be a more appropriate word. *Exploded* would have worked, except that I just used that one a bit earlier.

The stone blocks shook violently. The Alivened stumbled, the floor beneath it surging like waves on an ocean. Then the blocks dropped. They fell away before me, tumbling toward the level beneath. Bookshelves in the massive library room below were smashed as blocks of stone rained down, accompanied by an enormous paper monster.

The Alivened hit the ground, and there was a distinct shattering noise. It did not rise.

I spun wildly, dropping the last bits of the sword hilt. Sing was furiously reloading the shotgun. I brushed by him, charging the second Alivened. I reached to touch the ground, but the massive beast jumped, moving quickly out of the way. It was obviously smart enough to see what I had just done to its companion.

I raised a hand, slamming it into the jumping creature's chest. Then I released my Talent.

There was a strange, instant backlash — like hitting something solid with a baseball bat. I was thrown backward, my arm blazing with sudden pain.

The Alivened landed in a stumble. It stood for a moment, teetering. Then it exploded with a whooshing sound, a thousand crumpled sheets of paper erupting in an enormous, confetti-like burst.

I sat for a moment, staring. I blinked a few times, then lifted my hurt arm, wincing. Paper filled the corridor, bits fluttering around us.

"Wow," Sing said, standing up. He turned around, looking at the massive pit I had created. "Wow."

"I . . . didn't really do that intentionally," I said. "I just kind of let my power go, and that's what happened."

"I'll take it, either way," Sing said, resting the shotgun on his shoulder.

I climbed to my feet, shaking my arm. It didn't seem broken. "Bastille," I said, stumbling over to her. She was moving, fortunately, and as I arrived she groaned, then managed to sit up. Her jacket looked . . . shattered. Like the windshield of a car after it collides with a giant penguin.

Blasted giant penguins.

I tried to help Bastille to her feet, but she shook off my hands with annoyance. She stumbled a bit as she stood, then pulled off her jacket, looking at the spiderweb of lines. "Well, I guess that's useless now."

"Probably saved your life, Bastille," Sing said.

She shrugged, dropping it to the floor. It crackled like glass as it hit the stones.

"Your jacket was made of glass?" I asked, frowning.

"Of course," Bastille said. "Defender's Glass. Yours isn't?"

"Uh . . . no," I said.

"Then why wear something so atrocious?" she said, stumbling over to the hole in the floor. "You did this?" she asked, looking over at me.

I nodded.

"And . . . is that my sword down there, broken and shattered in a pile of books?"

"Afraid so," I said.

"Lovely," she grumbled.

"I was trying to save your life, Bastille," I said. "Which, I might point out, I *succeeded* in doing."

"Yeah, well, next time try not to bring down half the building when you do."

But I detected the barest hint of a smile on her lips when she said it.

CHAPTER 15

Moron.

It has been my experience that most problems in life are caused by a lack of information. Many people just don't know the things they need to know. Some ignore the truth; others never understand it.

When two friends get mad at each other, they usually do it because they lack information about each other's feelings. Americans lack information about Librarian control of their government. The people who pass this book on the shelf and don't buy it lack information about how wonderful, exciting, and useful it is.

Take, for instance, the word that started this chapter. You lacked information when you read it. You likely assumed that I was calling you an insulting name. You assumed wrong. *Moron* is actually a village in Switzerland located near the Jura mountain range. It's a nice place to live if you hate Librarians, for there is a well-hidden underground rebellion there.

Information. Perhaps you Hushlanders have read about Bastille and the others referring to guns as "primitive," and have been offended. Or, perhaps, you simply thought the text was being silly. In either case, maybe you should reevaluate.

The Free Kingdoms moved beyond the use of guns many centuries ago. The weapons became impractical for several reasons — some of which should be growing apparent from this narrative. Smedry Talents and Oculator abilities are not the only strange powers in the Free Kingdoms — and most of these abilities work better on items with large numbers of moving parts or breakable circuits. Using a gun against a Smedry, or one similarly talented, is usually a bad idea.

(This comes down to simple probability. The more that can go wrong with an item, the more that will. My computer — when I used to use one — was always about one click away from serious meltdown. My pencil, however, remains to this day remarkably virus-free.)

And so, many of the world's soldiers and warriors have moved on from guns, instead choosing weapons and armors created from Oculatory sands or silimatic technology. They don't often associate these items with their ancient counterparts — the people of the Free Kingdoms never got much beyond muskets before they moved on to using sand-based weapons — and so they think that guns are the primitive weapons. It makes sense, if you look at it from their perspective.

And anyone who's not willing to do that . . . well, they might just be a moron. Whether or not they live there.

"Sing, put those primitive guns away!" Bastille snapped, stepping away from the hole in the floor. "Those shattering things are so loud that half the library must have heard your racket!"

"They're effective, though," Sing said happily, changing the clips in a pair of his pistols. "They stopped that Alivened long enough for Alcatraz to take it down. I didn't see your sword doing half as well."

Bastille grumbled something, then paused, frowning. "Why is it so hot in here?"

I cursed, turning toward the glowing, smoking stones around the Firebringer's Lens. The floor looked dangerously close to becoming molten.

"I still can't believe old Smedry gave you a Firebringer's Lens," Bastille said. "That's like . . ."

"Giving a bazooka to a four-year-old?" I asked. I edged as close to the heated stones as I could stand. "That's kind of what I feel like when I pick the thing up."

"Well, turn it off!" Bastille said. "Quickly! You think Sing's guns were loud — using an Oculatory Lens that powerful will draw Blackburn's attention for certain. The longer you leave it on, the more loud it will seem!"

The reference to loudness probably doesn't make much sense to non-Oculators. After all, the Lens didn't make any noise. However, as I tried to figure out a way to turn off the Firebringer's Lens, I realized that I could *feel* it. Even though I'd only been aware of my Oculatory abilities for a short time, I was already getting in synch with them enough to sense when a powerful Lens was being used nearby.

The point is, I knew Bastille was right. I needed to turn that Lens off quickly. If Blackburn hadn't heard the gunfire, then he'd certainly notice the Lens "noise."

"Sing, loan me that shotgun," I said urgently, waving with my hand.

Sing reluctantly relinquished the weapon. As soon as

I touched it, the barrel fell off — but I was ready for that. I grabbed the tube of steel and used it to flip the Firebringer's Lens over. The Lens was convex, meaning it bulged out on one side, and now that it was flipped over it looked like a translucent eyeball staring up out of the ground. It continued to fire its superhot ray of light, which was now directed at the ceiling.

I used the barrel of the gun to scoot the Lens away from the heated section of the floor, then carefully reached out. I gritted my teeth — expecting to get burned — and touched the side of the Lens.

Remarkably (as I've mentioned before) the glass wasn't even hot. As soon as I touched it, the Lens shut off, the ray of light dwindling. I stepped back, surprised at how cold and dark the corridor now seemed by comparison.

"My shotgun," Sing said despondently as I handed back the barrel. "This was an antique!"

That's what happens when you stay around me, Sing, I thought with a sigh. *Things that you love get broken. Even when I don't do it on purpose.*

"Oh, get off it, Sing," Bastille said. "I lost my sword — you can't even *understand* how much trouble I'll be in for that. I was already bonded to the shattering thing; now I'll have to start the process all over, if they even let me. Next to that, your gun is nothing."

Sing sighed but nodded as Bastille reached into her handbag and pulled out a large, crystalline knife. You may, by the way, have noticed the connection between the word Crystin and the weapons made of crystal that Bastille uses. This is actually just a coincidence. Crystin is the Vendardi word for "grumpy," which all Crystins tend to be. And I think . . .

Nah, I'm just kidding. They got the name because they use crystal swords. Plus, they live in a big castle (dubbed Crystallia) made of — you guessed it — crystals. That clear enough? Crystal clear?

Ahem.

"I'm out of bullets for the Uzis too," Sing said, looking in his bag. "Small weapons for us both, I guess."

I knelt down and tentatively poked the Firebringer's Lens, still trying to pick it up off the floor. It began to glow. *Blast!* I thought and touched it again. The glow dissipated.

"Try being dumb," Bastille suggested.

"Excuse me?" I asked, frowning.

"Think dumb thoughts," Bastille said. "Or try not to think very much at all. The Lenses react to information and intelligence. So, it's easiest to handle them when there isn't much of either one around."

I paused. Then I frowned and looked at the Lens trying my best to be . . . well, stupid. I would like to note that this is quite a bit more difficult than it might sound. Particularly for a person like me, who can be (has this been mentioned?) rather clever.

Not only is it against a rashional purson's nature to try and convince himself that he is more stoopid than he thinks he is, it is quite dificult to not think about *anything* when one has been told not to. Only the trooly most briliant of peeple can purrtend stoopidity so sucessfuly.

Butt eet kan bee dun.

I closed my eyes and tried to empty my mind. Then I reached for the Lens. It started to glow. I frowned, then tapped it before it could go off.

"Maybe we should just leave it," Sing said nervously. "Before someone sees us."

"Too late," Bastille said, nodding down the hallway, to where a group of robed Librarians had just appeared around a corner. They looked quite anxious, and I suspected that

Bastille had been right in her earlier comment. The gunfire had been heard.

Bastille glanced at them through her sunglasses, then flipped her knife in her hand, raising it to throw.

"No!" I said. "Wait!"

Dutifully, she paused. The Librarians scattered, several racing back the way they had come.

"Why did you stop me?" Bastille asked testily.

"Those aren't paper monsters, Bastille," I said. "Those are unarmed people. We can't just kill them."

"We're at war, Alcatraz. Those people are the enemy. Plus, they're going to alert Blackburn!"

I shrugged. "It just didn't feel right. Besides, there were too many for you to kill them all. We can't keep our escape secret any longer."

Bastille snorted but otherwise fell silent. Either way, I didn't have any more time for acting stupid. I grabbed the Lens — it began to glow — and quickly shoved it back inside its velvet pouch. Then I reached in and tapped it off with a finger. I pulled the bag shut, then stuffed it in my pocket.

"Let's go, then," I said.

Bastille nodded. Sing, however, had moved over to the pile of ripped, shredded papers that were the remnants of the Alivened. "Alcatraz," he said. "There's something here you should see."

"What?" I asked, hurrying over. As I approached, I could see that in the center of the pile, Sing had found what appeared to be a portion of the Alivened that was still . . . well, *alive*ned.

It sat up as I arrived, causing Sing to point a pistol at it. The creature was smaller now, and it was much more human-shaped. However, it was still made of crumpled-up paper, and now that I was close, I could see that it had two beady, glasslike eyes.

I frowned, looking at Sing. "What's going on?"

"I don't know," Sing said. "Of course, I don't know a lot about Alivening. It's Dark Oculary."

"Why?" I asked, watching the three-foot-tall paper man with suspicious eyes.

"Bringing an inanimate thing to life this way is evil," Bastille said. "To do it, the Oculator has to give up a bit of his own humanity and store it in Glass of Alivening. That's what those eyes are made of. Shoot it, Sing. If you hit it in the eye, you might be able to kill it."

The little paper creature cocked its head, quizzically staring down the barrel of the gun.

I looked back at Bastille. "They give up a bit of their own humanity? What does that mean?"

"They let the glass drain them of things," Bastille explained.

"Things? That's specific."

From the side, I could see Bastille narrow her eyes behind her sunglasses, staring at the little creature with suspicion. "Human things, Alcatraz. Things like the capacity to love, protect others, and have mercy. Each time an Oculator creates an Alivened, he makes himself a little less human. Or, at least, he makes himself a little less like the kind of human the rest of us would want to associate with."

Sing nodded. "Most Dark Oculators think the transformation is an advantage." He reached down with his free hand, still keeping his gun leveled at the small Alivened. He held up a ripped bit of paper.

"You'd think that by giving up part of his humanity," the anthropologist said, "the Dark Oculator would create a creature that possessed good emotions. But that's not the way it works. The process twists the emotions, creating a creature that has just enough humanity to live, but not enough of it to really function."

I accepted the scrap of paper. I could read the text — it

appeared to be prose. The title line at the top right corner read *The Passionate Fire of Fiery Passion.*

"You can make an Alivened out of virtually anything," Sing said. "But substances that soak up emotion tend to work the best. That's why a lot of Dark Oculators prefer bad romance novels, since the object used determines the Alivened's temperament."

"Romance novels make an Alivened very violent," Bastille said. "But rather dense in the intelligence department."

"Go figure," I said, dropping the scrap of paper. *They give up their own humanity....* And this was the monster that had my grandfather held captive. "Come on," I said, standing. "We've wasted too much time already."

"And this thing?" Sing asked.

I paused. The Alivened looked up at me, its paper face somehow managing to convey a look of confusion.

I... broke it somehow, I thought. *I thought I'd killed it — but that's not the way my Talent works.* I don't destroy, not when the Talent is in full form. I just break and transform. "Leave it," I said.

Sing looked up in surprise.

"We don't want any more gunshots," I said. "Come on."

Sing shrugged, rising. Bastille moved down the hallway, checking the intersection. I quickly swapped my Oculator's Lenses for my Tracker's Lenses — fortunately, my grandfather's footprints were still glowing.

I didn't think I knew him that well, I thought.

I met Bastille at the intersection, pointing to the right branch. "Grandpa Smedry went that way."

"The same way the Librarians went," she said. "After they discovered us."

I nodded, glancing in the other direction. I pointed. "I see Ms. Fletcher's footprints that way."

"She turned away from the others?"

"No," I said. "She didn't go with Grandpa Smedry from the dungeons. Those footprints I can see now are the original ones we followed — the ones that led us to the place where we got captured. I told you we were close to where we started."

Bastille frowned. "How well do you know this Ms. Fletcher?"

I shrugged.

"It's been hours," Bastille said. "I'm surprised her footprints are still glowing."

I nodded. As I did, I noticed something else odd.

(If you haven't noticed, this is the chapter for noticing weird things. As opposed to the other chapters, in which only normal things were ever noticed. There is a story I could tell you about that, but as it involves eggbeaters, it is not appropriate for young people.)

The normalcy-challenged thing that I had noticed was actually not all that odd, all things considered. It was a lantern holder — the ornate bracket that I'd ripped free when I'd thrown the lantern at the Alivened.

There was nothing all that unusual about this lantern bracket, except for the already-noted fact that it was shaped like a cantaloupe. For all I knew, cantaloupe-shaped library lanterns were quite normal. Yet the sight of this one sparked a memory in my head. *Cantaloupe, fluttering paper makes a duck.*

I glanced back at the hallway behind me, with its broken wall, *more* broken floor, and piles of paper that shuffled in the draft.

It's probably nothing, I thought.

You, of course, know better than that.

CHAPTER 16

If you are anything like me — clever, fond of goat cheese, and devilishly handsome — then you have undoubtedly read many books. And, while reading those books, you likely have thought that you are smarter than the characters in those books.

You're just imagining things.

Now, I've already spoken about foreshadowing (a meddling literary convention of which Heisenberg would uncertainly be proud). However, there are other reasons why you only *think* that you're smarter than the characters in this book.

First off, you are likely sitting somewhere safe as you read the story. Whether it be a classroom, your bedroom, your aquarium, or even a library (but we won't get into that right now . . .), you have no need to worry about Alivened monsters, armed soldiers, or straw-fearing Gaks. Therefore, you can examine the events with a calm, unbiased eye. In such a state of mind, it is easy to find faults.

Secondly, you have the convenience of holding this story in book form. It is a complete narrative, which you can look through at your leisure. You can go back and reread sections (which, because of the marvelous writing the book contains, you have undoubtedly already done). You could even scan to the end and read the last page. Know that by doing so, however, you would violate every holy and honorable story-telling principle known to man, thereby throwing the universe into chaos and causing grief to untold millions.

Your choice.

Either way, since you can reread anytime you want, you could go back and find out *exactly* where I first heard canta-loupes mentioned. With such an advantage, it is very easy to find and point out things that my friends and I originally missed.

The third reason you think you are smarter than the characters is because you have me to explain things to you. Obviously, you don't fully appreciate this advantage. Suffice it to say that without me, you would be far more confused about this story than you are. In fact, without me, you'd probably be *very* confused as you tried to read this book.

After all, it would be filled with blank pages.

Two soldiers stood in the hallway, chatting with each other, obviously guarding the door that sat between them. Sing, Bastille, and I crouched around a corner just a short distance away, unnoticed. We'd followed Grandpa Smedry's footprints all the way here. His prints went through the door — and that, therefore, was the way we needed to go.

I nodded to Bastille, and she slipped quietly around the corner, moving with such grace that she resembled an ice-skater on the smooth stone floor. The guards looked over as she approached, but she was so quick that they didn't have time to cry out. Bastille elbowed one in the teeth, then caught his companion in a grip around the neck, choking him and keeping him quiet. The first guard stumbled, holding his mouth, and Bastille kicked him in the chest.

The first guard fell to the ground, hitting his head and going unconscious. She dropped the second guard a moment later, after he'd passed out from being choked. She hadn't even needed the dagger.

"You really *are* good at this," I whispered as I approached.

Bastille shrugged modestly as I moved up to the door. Sing followed me, looking over his shoulder down the hallway, anxious.

I knew it wouldn't be long before the entire library was on alert. We didn't have much time. I didn't care about the Sands of Rashid. I just wanted to get my grandfather back.

"His footprints go under the door," I whispered.

"I know," Bastille whispered as she peeked through a crack in the door. "He's still in there."

"What?" I said, kneeling beside her.

"Alcatraz!" Bastille hissed. "Blackburn's in there too."

I paused beside the door, peeking through an open-holed knot in the wood. That was one thing that old-style wooden doors had over the more refined American versions. In fact, Bastille would probably have called this door more 'advanced,' since it had the advantage of holes you could look through.

The view in the room was exactly what I had feared. Grandpa Smedry lay strapped to a large table, his shirt removed. Blackburn stood in his suit a short distance away, an angry expression on his face. I twisted a bit, looking to the side. Quentin was there too, tied to a chair. The short, dapper man looked like he'd been beaten a bit — his nose was bleeding, and he seemed dazed. I could hear him muttering.

"Bubble gum for the primate. Long live the Jacuzzi. Moon on the rocks, please."

The walls of the room were covered with various nasty-looking torture implements — the kinds of things one might find in a dentist's office. If that dentist were an *insane, torture-hungry Dark Oculator.*

And there were also . . . "Books?" I whispered in confusion.

Bastille shuddered. "Papercuts," she said. "The worst form of torture."

Of course, I thought.

"Alcatraz," Bastille said. "You have to leave. Blackburn will see your aura again!"

"No he won't," I said, smiling.

"Why not?"

"Because he made the same mistake I did before," I said. "He's not wearing his Oculator's Lens."

Indeed he wasn't. In his single, monocled eye, Blackburn was *not* wearing his Oculator's Lens. Instead, as I had anticipated, he was wearing a Torturer's Lens — it was easy to distinguish, with its dark green and black tints.

Perhaps I wasn't as stupid as you thought.

"Ah," Bastille said.

Blackburn turned, focusing on Grandpa Smedry. Even though I wasn't wearing my Oculator's Lenses, I could feel a release of power — the Dark Oculator was activating the Torturer's Lens. *No!* I thought, feeling helpless, remembering the awful pain.

Grandpa Smedry lay with a pleasant expression on his face. "I say," he said. "I don't suppose I could bother you for a cup of milk? I'm getting a bit thirsty."

"Turtlenecks look good when the trees have no ears," Quentin added.

"Bah!" Blackburn said. "Answer my questions, old man! How do I bypass the Sentinel's Glass of Ryshadium? How can I grow the crystals of Crystallia?" He released another burst of torturing power into Grandpa Smedry.

"I really need to get going," Grandpa Smedry said. "I'm late — I don't suppose we could call it a day?"

Blackburn screamed in frustration, taking off his Torturer's Lens and looking at it with an annoyed eye. "You!" he snapped to a guard that I couldn't see.

"Uh . . . yes, my lord?" a voice asked.

"Stand right there," Blackburn said, putting on the monocle. I sensed another wave of power.

The guard screamed. I couldn't see him crumple, but I could hear it — and I could hear the pain, the utter agony, in the poor man's voice. I cringed, closing my eyes and gritting my teeth against the awful sound as I remembered that brief moment when I had felt Blackburn's fury.

I had to work hard to keep myself from fleeing right then. But I stayed. I'll point out that now, looking back, I don't consider this bravery — just stupidity.

The guard stopped screaming, then began to whimper.

"Hmm," Blackburn said. "The Lens works perfectly. Your Talent is stronger than I had anticipated, old man. But it can't protect you forever! Soon you'll know the pain!"

Bastille suddenly grabbed my arm — she was still watching through the crack beside me. "He's arriving late for the pain!" she said in an excited whisper. "Such power . . . to put off an abstract sensation. It's amazing."

I noted the look of relief in Bastille's face. *She does care,* I realized. *Despite all the grumbling, despite all the complaints. She really was worried about him.*

"What's going on?" Sing whispered. He was too big to fit beside the door with the two of us.

"Old Smedry is handling the torture with poise," Bastille said. "But Quentin looks like he's had a hard time."

"Is he babbling?" Sing asked.

Bastille nodded.

"Then he's gone into anti-information mode," Sing said. "He can engage his Talent so that it translates *everything* he says into gibberish. He can't turn it off, even if he wants to — not until it wears off a day later."

"That's why he makes such a good spy," I realized. "He can't betray secrets — they can't force him to talk, no matter how hard they try!"

Sing nodded.

Inside the room, Blackburn stomped around the table. He grabbed a knife from a rack of torturing implements, then rammed it toward Grandpa Smedry's leg.

It missed, sliding just to the side, and Blackburn swore in frustration. He held the knife up, steadied his hand, then carefully plunged it down again.

This time, it hit Grandpa's leg and jabbed directly into the flesh.

"Shattered Glass," Bastille cursed. "The knife is too advanced a weapon — it can get past old Smedry's Talent."

I stared in shock at the cut in my grandfather's leg. No blood came out, however.

"It's a good thing I don't need to go to the bathroom,"

Grandpa Smedry said in a cheerful voice. "That would be embarrassing, wouldn't it?"

"We have to do something," Bastille said urgently. "He's powerful, but he can't hold back the pain — or the wounds — forever."

"But we can't fight a Dark Oculator," Sing said. "Especially not without your sword, Bastille."

I stood. "Then we'll have to get him to leave Grandpa alone. Come on!" With that, I rushed down the hallway. Bastille and Sing followed in a dash.

"Alcatraz!" Bastille said as soon as we were a safe distance from the torture room. "What are you planning?"

"We need a distraction," I said. "Something that will draw Blackburn away long enough for us to get in and rescue Grandpa Smedry. And I think I know of one."

Bastille was about to object, but at that moment Sing tripped. Bastille and I ducked to the side just as a pair of bow-tied, sword-carrying Librarian soldiers came up out of the stairwell ahead. Bastille cursed, dashing toward them with a sudden burst of Crystin speed.

The stairs they had come up were the very same stairs that we ourselves had come up a few hours before. That meant the door I wanted was —

I threw my weight against it, pushing open the door and stepping into a room filled with caged dinosaurs.

"Good day!" said Charles. "I see that you have not ended up dead. What a pleasant surprise!"

"Did you bring us something to eat?" the Tyrannosaurus asked hopefully.

"Better," I said, then rushed into the room, touching the cage locks as I moved. Each one my fingers brushed against snapped open, the complicated gears inside breaking easily before my Talent.

"Why, what a good chap you are!" Charles said. The group of twenty dinosaurs agreed with eager, loud voices.

"I've freed you," I said. "But I need something in return. Can you cause a disturbance downstairs for me?"

"Of course, my good fellow!" Charles said. "We're *excellent* at creating disturbances, aren't we, George?"

"Indeed, indeed!" said the Stegosaurus.

With that, I stepped aside, waving eagerly, trying to begin a stampede of undersized dinosaurs. They, of course, filed out of the room in a very gentlemanly manner — for, as everyone knows, all British are refined, calm, and well-mannered. Even if they are a bunch of dinosaurs.

I followed the group out of the room, trying to whip them into a frenzy — or at least a mild agitation.

"*That's* your plan?" Bastille asked flatly, standing above two unconscious Librarians.

"They'll make a disturbance," I said. "I mean, they're *dinosaurs.*"

Bastille and Sing shared a look.

"What?" I said. "Don't you think it'll work?"

"You know very little about dinosaurs, Alcatraz," Bastille said as the dinosaurs went down the stairs to the first floor.

We waited. We waited for painful minutes, hiding in the Forgotten Language room. We heard no cries of panic. No yells for help. No sounds of people being chewed up by rampaging, bloodthirsty reptiles.

"Oh, for goodness' sake!" I said, rushing from the room and running over to the hallway with the broken floor. I got on my hands and knees and peered through the opening, hoping to catch a glimpse of chaos below.

Instead, I saw the dinosaurs sitting in a group, several stacks of books settled around them. One of them — the Stegosaurus — appeared to be reading to the others.

"Dinosaurs," Bastille said. "Useless."

"They are easily distracted by books, Alcatraz," Sing said. "I don't think they're going to help much."

"Hey!" I called with an annoyed voice. "Charles."

The little Pterodactyl looked up. "Ah, my good friend!"

"What about the chaos?" I demanded.

"Done!" Charles said.

"We each moved six books out of their proper places," called George the Stegosaurus. "It will take them *days* to find them all and put them back."

"Though we did put them into place backward," Charles said. "You know, so they could be seen more easily. We wouldn't want it to be *too* hard."

"Too hard?" I asked, stupefied. "Charles, these are the people who were going to kill you and bury your bones in an archaeological dig!"

"Well, that's no reason to be uncivilized!" Charles said.

"Indeed!" called a duck-billed dinosaur.

I knelt, blinking.

"Dinosaurs," Bastille said again. "Useless."

"Don't worry, my Oculator friend!" Charles called. "We gave them a little extra kick! We had Douglas eat the science fiction section!"

"Well," admitted Douglas the T. Rex, "I only ate the 'C'

section. Honestly — claiming that Velociraptors were the smartest dinosaurs? I knew a Velociraptor in college, and he *failed* chemistry. Plus, resurrecting a character just because he didn't die in the movie? Poppycock, I say!"

I sat back. Bastille had the dignity not to say, "I told you so." Or, at least, she had the dignity not to say it a third time.

We need another plan. Another plan. Can't stop to think about the failure. We need to draw the Dark Oculator away. Need to . . .

I stood, steeling my nerves.

"Another idea?" Sing asked, clearly a little apprehensive.

I took off again. Sing and Bastille followed reluctantly. But they hadn't come up with anything better. My failure with the dinosaurs had come from relying on misinformation. In most books, two dozen rampaging dinosaurs would have been a distraction worthy of even a Dark Oculator's attention.

That's why most books aren't true. Sorry, kids.

I dashed back toward the torturing room. The guards still lay unconscious in the hallway where Bastille had left them. I checked the knothole — Blackburn was still there inside, and he had apparently decided to rough up Grandpa Smedry with slaps to the face.

"I think I'll go for a walk. . . ." Grandpa Smedry said cheerfully.

"Wasing not of wasing is," Quentin added.

I gritted my teeth. Then I pulled the velvet pouch out of my pocket and looked inside.

"Alcatraz . . ." Bastille said carefully. "You can't defeat him. You might have a powerful Lens, but that's not everything. Blackburn will be able to deflect that Firebringer's Lens with his Oculator's Lens."

"I know," I said. "Sing, take these two unconscious men and hide them — with yourself — in the Forgotten Language room."

My cousin opened his mouth as if to object, but then paused. Finally, he nodded. He easily lifted the two unconscious men, then left down the hallway.

"Alcatraz," Bastille said. "I know you want to protect your grandfather. But this is suicide."

I waited a few moments for Sing to complete his task. Then I knelt down beside the door and looked through the knothole. Blackburn was raising a mallet, as if to break Grandpa Smedry's arm.

"You can't resist forever, old man," Blackburn said.

I activated the Firebringer's Lens.

CHAPTER 17

Immediately, the Dark Oculator looked up.

I smiled, watching Blackburn turn with a confused expression on his face. At that moment, he was sensing a very powerful Oculatory Lens coming in from the hallway outside. He took a step toward the door.

"Now," I hissed. "*Run!*"

Bastille didn't need further command. She took off down the hallway, as did I. However, she obviously held back so that she didn't outstrip me.

I held the Firebringer's Lens before me, and it spewed forth its powerful line of light. I ran on, aiming it at the side of the corridor.

"You're leading him away!" Bastille said. "You're using us as bait."

"Hopefully bait that escapes," I said, ducking around a corner, then pausing to wait. The Firebringer's Lens continued to blast.

A door slammed in the distance. "Smedry!" a voice bellowed. "You can't run from me! Don't you realize that I can sense your power?"

"Go!" I said, taking off at a dash. Within seconds, we were at the section of the corridor with the broken floor.

"Charles!" I yelled down through the hole. "Trouble is coming your way! I'd run, if I were you!"

And then I took the Firebringer's Lens and tossed it through the hole. It bounced against a few books, then came to rest on the floor, still shooting a piercing-hot laser of heat up into the air, burning the ceiling, threatening to start several of the bookshelves on fire.

I grabbed Bastille by the arm, tugging her around the corner and into the Forgotten Language room. Sing jumped as we entered. He had — for some reason that he never explained — propped both of the unconscious men in chairs at the desks.

Anthropologists are funny that way.

Now, I would like to take this opportunity to point out

that I didn't take the opportunity to point out anything at the beginning of this chapter. Never fear; my editorial comments were simply delayed for a few moments.

You see, that last chapter ended with a terribly unfair hook. By now, it is probably very late at night, and you have stayed up to read this book when you *should* have gone to sleep. If this is the case, then I commend you for falling into my trap. It is a writer's greatest pleasure to hear that someone was kept up until the unholy hours of the morning reading one of his books. It goes back to authors being terrible people who delight in the suffering of others. Plus, we get a kickback from the caffeine industry.

Regardless, because of how exciting things were, I didn't feel comfortable interjecting my normal comments at the beginning of this chapter. So, I shall put them here instead. Prepare yourself.

Blah, blah, sacrifice, altars, daggers, sharks. Blah, blah, something pretentious. Blah, blah, rutabaga. Blah, blah, something that makes no sense whatsoever.

Now back to the story.

(And whoever put in that cliff-hanger at the end of the last chapter needs to be reprimanded. It's growing quite late here, and I really should be getting to bed, rather than writing this book.)

I crouched inside the Forgotten Language room with Bastille and Sing. I kept my Oculator's Lenses off, hoping that without them I wouldn't have as strong an aura. Sure enough, watching under the door, we saw a dark shadow pass by, and I felt a slight surge of power as an activated Oculatory Lens passed by. (Fortunately, Blackburn didn't appear to have a Tracker's Lens of his own.) His shadow didn't stop to check the Forgotten Language room, but instead continued on toward the stairwell.

"We have very little time," I said, looking back at the other two.

We burst from the room and ran back toward the torture chamber. By the time we arrived, I was feeling a little out of breath. Having never had to rescue anyone from torture before, I wasn't accustomed to so much running. Fortunately, Sing wasn't exactly in shape either, and so I didn't feel *too* bad lagging behind Bastille.

Once I reached the guard chamber, I noticed Bastille standing beside the door with the peephole. She gave the handle a good rattle. "Locked," she said.

"Move aside," I said, walking up to the door. I rested a

hand on the lock, jolting it with a bit of Breaking Talent. Nothing happened.

"Glass lock," I said. I moved my hand up to the door's hinges, but they resisted too.

Bastille cursed. "The whole door will be warded against your Talent. We'll have to try to break it down manually."

I eyed the thick wooden door with a skeptical eye. Then, from behind me, there was a click. I turned to see Sing leveling one of the biggest, baddest handguns I'd ever seen. It was the kind of gun that took most men two hands to hold — the type of gun that used bullets so big that they could have doubled as paperwcights.

Sing pulled out another gun, identical to the first, in his other hand. Then he took aim at the door handle — which sat directly between Bastille and me.

"Oh, put those antiques away," Bastille said testily. "This isn't the time for — Gak!"

This last part came as I grabbed her by the shoulder, yanking her with me as I took cover behind a table.

Sing pulled the triggers.

Wood chips sprayed across the room, mixing with shards of dark black glass. The booming sound of gunshots echoed in the small chamber — or, at least, the booming sound of *three* gunshots echoed in the small chamber. By the time Sing fired the fourth shot, I'd been deafened and couldn't tell whether or not the rest of the shots made any noise.

I couldn't hear any trees fall either.

When it was over, I peeked out from behind my table. Bastille remained stunned on the floor beside me. The door stood shattered and splintered, the remnants of its handle and lock hanging pitifully, surrounded by bullet holes. As I watched, the broken, bullet-shattered lock finally dropped to the floor, and the door quietly swung open — as if in surrender.

Now, after all our discussions of "advanced" weapons and the like, you probably weren't expecting the guns to do much good. I certainly wasn't. One thing to remember is this: Primitive doesn't always mean useless. An old flintlock pistol may not be as advanced as a handgun, but both could kill you. Sitting there, I realized why Sing was insistent upon bringing the guns along, and why Grandpa Smedry had let him do so.

It seems to me that some people underestimate good, old-fashioned Hushlander technology a little too much. It was good to see something from my world prove so effective. Locks made from Oculator's Glass might be *resistant* to physical damage, but they certainly aren't completely indestructible.

"Nice shooting," I said.

Sing shrugged, then said something.

"What?" I asked, still feeling a bit deaf.

"I said," Sing said, speaking louder, "even *antiques* have their uses every once in a while. Come on!" He waddled over to the door, pushing it open the rest of the way.

Bastille stumbled to her feet. "I feel like a thunderstorm went off inside my head. Your people really use those things on the battlefield?"

"Only when they have to," I said.

"How can you hear what your commanders are saying?" she asked.

"Uh . . . helmets?" I said. The answer, of course, didn't make any sense. But I didn't care at the moment. I rose to my feet, rushing after Sing into the room. Inside, we found one guard on the ground, unconscious from Blackburn's use of the Torturer's Lens. Grandpa Smedry still lay tied to the table, Quentin in his chair.

"Alcatraz, lad!" Grandpa Smedry said. "You're late!"

I smiled, rushing to the table. Bastille saw to Quentin, cutting the ropes that tied him to the chair.

"The manacles on my wrists are made of Enforcer's Glass, lad," Grandpa Smedry said. "You'll never break it. Quickly, you have to leave! The Dark Oculator sensed you using the Firebringer's Lens!"

"I know," I said. "That was intentional. We distracted him with the Lens, then came in to get you."

"You did?" Grandpa Smedry said. "Whooping Williams, lad, that's brilliant!"

"Thank you," I said, placing two hands against the wood of the table. Then I closed my eyes and channeled a blast of Talent into it. Fortunately, it wasn't warded as well as the door had been, even if the manacles were. Nails sprang free, boards separated, and legs fell off. Grandpa Smedry collapsed in the middle of it, crying out in surprise. Sing quickly rushed over to help him to his feet.

"Muttering Modesitts," Grandpa Smedry said quietly, looking at the remnants of the table. The manacles and their chains now hung freely from his wrists and ankles, for the other ends had been affixed to the now-defunct table.

Grandpa Smedry looked up at me. "That's some Talent, lad. Some Talent indeed . . ."

Quentin walked over, rubbing his wrists. He had a few budding bruises on his face, but otherwise looked unharmed. "Churches," he said. "Lead, very small rocks, and ducks."

I frowned.

"Oh, he won't be able to say anything normal for the rest of the day," Grandpa Smedry said. "Sing, my boy, would you help me with . . ." He nodded downward, toward his leg — which, I now noticed, was still impaled by the torturing knife.

"Grandpa!" I said with concern as Sing reached down gingerly and pulled the knife free.

There was no blood.

"Don't worry, lad," Grandpa Smedry said. "I'll arrive late to that wound."

I frowned. "How long can you keep that up?"

"It depends," Grandpa Smedry said, accepting his tuxedo shirt from Sing. He put it on, then began doing up the front. "Arriving late to wounds requires a bit of effort — holding this one back, along with all the pains

Blackburn gave me with his Torturer's Lenses, is already fatiguing. I can hold on for a little while longer, but I'll have to start letting the pain through eventually."

Indeed, Grandpa Smedry looked far less spry now than he had earlier in the day. The torture might not have broken him, but it had certainly produced an effect.

"Oh, don't look at me like that," Grandpa Smedry said. "I can arrive at the pain in small, manageable amounts, once we're free. Bastille, dear, any luck?"

I turned. Bastille had apparently done a quick search of the room's tables and cabinets. She looked up from the last one and shook her head. "If he took your Lenses, he didn't stash them in here, old man."

"Ah, well," Grandpa Smedry said. "Good work anyway, dear."

"I only searched the room," she said, slamming the door, "because I was so *furious* at you for getting yourself captured. I figured that if I walked over to help you, I'd end up punching you instead. That didn't seem fair in your weakened state."

Grandpa Smedry raised a hand, whispering to me, "This would probably be a bad time to remind her that *she* got captured too, eh?"

"My capture was a *different* Smedry's fault," Bastille snapped, flushing. "And that doesn't matter. We need to get out of here before that Dark Oculator comes back."

"Agreed," Grandpa Smedry said. "Follow me — I know the way to a stairwell up."

"*Up?*" Bastille asked incredulously.

"Of course," Grandpa Smedry said. "We came for the Sands of Rashid — and we're not leaving until we have them!"

"But they know we're here," Bastille said. "The entire library is on alert!"

"Yes," Grandpa Smedry said. "But *we* know where the sands are."

"We do?" I asked.

Grandpa Smedry nodded. "You don't think Quentin and I got ourselves captured for nothing, do you? We got close to the sands, lad. Very close."

"But?" Bastille asked, folding her arms.

Grandpa Smedry blushed slightly. "Snarer's Glass. Blackburn has that room so well trapped that it's a wonder he doesn't catch himself every time he walks into it."

"And how are we going to get past the traps now, then?" Bastille asked.

"Oh, we won't have to," Grandpa Smedry said. "Quentin and I couldn't think of a way to get by the traps, so we just fell into them! The room should be completely free now. Each square of Snarer's Glass can only go off once, you know!"

Bastille huffed at him. "You could have gotten yourself killed, old man!"

"Yes, well," he said. "I didn't! Now, let's get moving! We're going to be late."

With that, he rushed out of the room. Bastille gave me a flat look. "Next time, let's just leave him."

I smiled wryly, moving to follow her out of the room. However, something caught my attention. I stopped beside it.

"Sing?" I asked as the large man walked past.

"Yes?"

I pointed at a lantern holder on the wall. "What does this lantern holder look like to you?"

Sing paused, scratching his chin. "A coconut?"

Coconut, I thought. "Do you remember what Quentin said downstairs, just after we entered the library?"

Sing shook his head. "What was it?"

"I can't quite remember," I said. "But it sounded like gibberish."

"Ah," Sing said. "Quentin speaks in gibberish sometimes. It's a side effect of his Talent — like me tripping when I get startled."

Or me breaking things I don't want to, I thought. But this seemed different. *Coconuts,* Quentin had said. *Coconuts . . . pain don't hurt. That's what it was.*

I glanced back at the broken table. The pain of torture hadn't hurt Grandpa Smedry.

"Come on, Alcatraz," Sing said urgently, pulling on my arm. "We have to keep moving."

I allowed myself to be led from the room, but not before I took one last look at the wall bracket.

I had the feeling that I was missing something important.

CHAPTER 18

The book is almost done.

The ending of a book is, in my experience, both the best and the *worst* part to read. For the ending will often decide whether you love or hate the book.

Both emotions lead to disappointment. If the ending was good, and the book was worth your time, then you are left annoyed and depressed because there is no more book to read. However, if the ending was bad, then it's too late to stop reading. You're left annoyed and depressed because you wasted so much time on a book with a bad ending.

Therefore, reading is obviously worthless, and you should go spend your time on other, more valuable pursuits. I hear that algebra is good for you. Kind of like humility, plus factoring. Regardless, you will soon know whether to hate me for not writing more, or whether to hate me for writing too much. Please confine all assassination attempts to the school week, as I would rather not die on a Saturday.

No need to spoil a good weekend.

"This is it," Grandpa Smedry said, leading us through another hallway. "That door at the end."

The third floor was a little more lavish than the second floor: Instead of stark, unpleasant stones and blank walls, the third floor was lined with stark, unpleasant rugs and blank tapestries. The door had a large glass disc set into its front, and at first I thought the disc had a lightbulb in the middle. It certainly glowed sharply enough. Then I remembered my Oculator's Lenses and realized that the disc was glowing only to my eyes.

There had to be Lenses beyond that door — powerful ones.

Bastille caught Grandpa Smedry on the shoulder as he reached the door, then shook her head sharply. She pulled him back, moved up to the door, and tried to get a good look through the glass disc. Then she raised her crystal dagger to the ready and pushed open the door.

Light burst from the room, as if that door were the gate to heaven itself. I cried out, closing my eyes.

"Focus on your Lenses, lad," Grandpa Smedry said. "You can dim the effect if you concentrate."

I did so, squinting. I managed, with some effort, to make the light dim down until it was a low glow. No longer blinded, I was awed by what I saw.

What I felt at this point is a little bit hard to describe. To Bastille and my cousins, the room would have been simply a medium-sized, circular chamber with little shelves built into the walls. The shelves held Lenses — hundreds of them — and each one had its own little stand, holding it up to sparkle in the light. It must have been a pretty sight, but nothing spectacular.

To me, the room looked *different.*

Perhaps you've owned something in your life to which you ascribed particular pleasure. A treasured toy, perhaps. Some photographs. The bullet that killed your archnemesis.

Now, imagine that you'd never before realized how important that item was to you. Imagine that your understanding of it — your feelings of love, pride, and satisfaction — suddenly hit you all at once.

This was how I felt. There was something *right* about all of those Lenses. I'd never been in the room before, but to me, it felt like home. And to a boy who had lived with dozens of different foster families, *home* was not a word to be used lightly.

Sing, Grandpa Smedry, Bastille, and Quentin moved into the room. I walked up to the doorway, where I stood for a few moments, basking in the beauty of the Lenses. There was a majesty to the room. A warmth.

This is what I was meant to be, I thought. *This was what I was always meant to be.*

"Hurry, lad!" Grandpa Smedry said. "You have to find the sands. I don't have my Oculator's Lenses! I'll try to find a pair in here, but you need to start looking while I do!"

I shocked myself into motion. We were still being chased. This wasn't my home — this was the stronghold of my enemies. I shook my head, forcing myself to be more realistic. Yet I would always retain a memory of that moment — the first moment when I knew for certain that I wanted to be an Oculator. And I would treasure it.

"Grandfather, *everything* in here is glowing," I protested. "How can I find the sands in all of this?"

"They're here," Grandpa Smedry said, furiously looking through the room. "I swear they are!"

"Golf the spasm of penguins!" Quentin said, pointing to a table at the back of the circular room.

"He's right!" Grandpa Smedry said. "That's where the sands were before. Aspiring Asimovs! Where did they go?"

"Typically," a new voice said, "one uses sands to make Lenses."

I spun. Blackburn stood in the hallway behind us. For some reason, the man's aura of darkness was far less visible than it had been before.

My Oculator's Lenses, I realized. *I turned them down.*

Blackburn smiled. He was accompanied by a large group of Librarians — not the skinny, robe-wearing kind but the bulky, overmuscled kind in the bow ties and sunglasses, as well a couple of sword-wielding women wearing skirts, their hair in buns.

Blackburn had something in his hand. A pair of spectacles. Even with my Oculator's Lenses turned down, these spectacles glowed powerfully with a brilliant white light.

"Back away, lad," Grandpa Smedry said quietly.

I did so, slowly backing into the room. *There are no other exits*, I thought. *We're trapped!*

Bastille growled quietly, raising her crystal dagger, stepping between Grandpa Smedry and the smiling Blackburn. Librarian thugs fanned into the room, moving to surround us. Sing watched warily, cocking a pair of handguns.

"Nice collection you have here, Blackburn," Grandpa Smedry said, walking around the perimeter of the room. "Frostbringer's Lenses, Courier's Lenses, Harrier's Lenses ... Yes, impressive indeed." I noticed that my grandfather's hand was glowing slightly.

"I have a weakness for power, I'm afraid," Blackburn said.

Grandpa Smedry nodded, as if to himself. "Those Lenses in your hand. They come from the Sands of Rashid?"

Blackburn smiled.

"Why a pair? Why not just a monocle?" Grandpa Smedry asked.

"In case I choose to share these Lenses with others. Not everyone has realized the value of focusing power, as I have."

"The torture, the chasing us," Grandpa Smedry said. "I was worried that we were taking too long — that you were just trying to distract us long enough for your lackeys to forge those Lenses."

"Not *just*," Blackburn said. "I was sincerely hoping that I'd be able to break you with the torture, old man, and find the secret to the Smedry Talents that way. But you do have a point. I assumed that when I had these Lenses, I could beat you for certain."

Grandpa Smedry smiled. "They don't do what you thought they would, do they?"

Blackburn shrugged.

Grandpa Smedry finally stopped strolling. He reached up and selected a Lens off of a shelf, then slipped it into his hand with several others he'd pilfered. He turned to look directly at Blackburn. "Shall we, then?"

Blackburn's smile deepened. "I'd like nothing better."

Grandpa Smedry whipped his hand up, raising something to his eye — an Oculator's Lens. Blackburn raised his own hand, placing a monocle *over* the one he already wore.

Sing, of course, tripped.

"Shattering Glass!" Bastille swore, grabbing me by the arm and towing me to the side. The Librarian thugs all stooped down, bracing themselves.

And the air suddenly began to crackle with energy. My hair raised up on its ends, and each footstep zapped me slightly with a static charge.

"What's going on?" I cried to Bastille.

"Oculators' Duel!" she said.

I noticed Grandpa Smedry raise another Lens to his eye. He kept his left eye closed, placing both lenses together over his right eye. The first Lens he had placed — the reddish-pink Oculator's Lens — remained in place, hovering in front of his eye.

Blackburn raised a third Lens to his eye. The room surged with power, and Lenses on the walls started to rattle. I recognized this one — it was a Torturer's Lens. I could feel that it had been activated, yet it seemed to have no effect on Grandpa Smedry.

"Those Oculator's Lenses you wear," Bastille said over the noise. "They're the most basic Lenses for a good reason. A well-trained Oculator can use them to negate his enemy's attacks."

Grandpa Smedry slowly raised a third Lens to his eye. All three remained hovering in the air in front of him. The new one made a screeching sound that hurt my ears, though most of the noise seemed directed at Blackburn.

"Why are they using multiple Lenses at once?" I said as Blackburn added a fourth Lens. The room grew colder, and a line of frosty ice shot forward toward Grandpa Smedry.

Bastille crouched down farther. Wind began to churn in the room, ruffling my hair, whipping at my jacket.

"They're countering each other's attacks," Bastille said. "Adding Lens after Lens. However, it gets increasingly hard to focus your power through all those Lenses at once. The first one who loses control of his Lenses — or who fails to block an attack — will lose."

Grandpa Smedry, arm beginning to shake, raised a fourth Lens to his eye. The hovering line of Lenses trembled in the wind. Grandpa Smedry was no longer smiling — in fact, he had one arm up, steadying himself against the wall.

Blackburn added a fifth Lens — one that I recognized. It didn't have a little monocle frame like the others, and it had a red dot at the center.

My Firebringer's Lens! I thought. *He* did *recover it.*

Sure enough, this Lens began to spit out a line of fire. The beam shot forward, moving alongside the line of ice. But, like the ice line, the Firebringer's line puffed into non-existence near Grandpa Smedry, as if hitting an invisible shield. Grandpa Smedry grunted quietly at the impact.

I could see Sing a short distance away, struggling to his knees. The large man raised a gun, then fired at Blackburn. I could barely hear the gunshots over the sound of wind.

Flashes of lightning shot from Blackburn's body, moving more quickly than I could track. I'm still not certain what happened to those bullets, but they obviously never reached their mark. I glanced at Sing, who sat cradling a burned hand, his gun smoking slightly on the floor.

Grandpa Smedry finally managed to place his fifth Lens. My ears popped, and it felt like the air was growing more pressurized — as if some force were pushing out from Grandpa Smedry, most of it slamming into Blackburn.

The Dark Oculator grunted, stumbling. However, I could see a glistening spot appear near the knife-hole on Grandpa Smedry's tuxedo pants, and a small pool of blood began forming at his feet.

The wound from the torture chamber, I thought. *He's too tired to hold it back any longer.* "We have to do something!" I yelled over the wind. Lenses were toppling from their pedestals, some shattering to the ground, and scraps of paper were churning inside the vortex of the room.

Bastille shook her head. "We can't interfere!"

"What?" I asked. "Some stupid code of honor?"

"No! If we get too close to either of them, the power will vaporize us!"

Oh, I thought. Blackburn, whose arm had begun to tremble with strain, raised a sixth Lens to his eye. In his hand, he still held the spectacles he'd had forged from the Sands of Rashid. *Why doesn't he use those?* I wondered. *Is he saving the best for last?*

Sing managed to pull himself over to Bastille and me.

"Lord Leavenworth can't win this fight, Bastille! He's only using single-eye Lenses. Blackburn's trained on those — he put his eye out to increase his power with them. But Leavenworth is accustomed to two eyes. He can't —"

Grandpa Smedry suddenly let out a defiant yell. He raised his hand, gripping his sixth Lens in rigid fingers. He wavered for a moment.

Then dropped the Lens.

There was a flash of light and a blast of power. I cried out in shock as I was thrown backward.

And the winds stopped.

I opened my eyes to the sound of laughter. I rolled over, desperately looking for Grandpa Smedry. The old man lay on the ground, barely moving. Blackburn had been thrown backward as well, but he picked himself up without much trouble.

"Is that it?" Blackburn asked, brushing off his suit. He smiled, looking down at Grandpa Smedry through his single eye, an eye that now bore no Lenses. They had all dropped to the ground at his feet. "You barely gave a fight, old man."

Sing reached for another gun. Two beefy Librarians tackled him from behind. Bastille jumped the first one. Six more soldiers rushed at her.

Blackburn continued to chuckle. He walked slowly across the room, his feet crunching on shattered glass. He shook his head. "Do you realize how much trouble it's going to be to gather up all these broken Lenses, have the shards sorted, then have them all reforged? My Librarians will spend months remaking my collection!"

I have to do something, I thought. Bastille continued to fight, but more and more Librarian thugs were surrounding her. They already had Quentin and Sing pinned. Nobody, however, seemed to notice me. Perhaps they thought me unthreatening because I had been knocked down.

I scanned the room. There, a short distance away, I saw them — the Lenses of Rashid, lying temptingly in the middle of a pile of discarded monocles. They had fallen to the ground during the blast along with the other Lenses Blackburn had held during the fight.

I gritted my teeth.

I have to use the Lenses of Rashid, I thought, crawling forward slowly. *I have to —*

Wait. I want you to do something for me. Try to recall the very *first* part of my story. It was way back in Chapter One, before I even told you about my name. Back then, I spoke about life-and-death situations, and how they make people think about some very odd subjects. The prospect of dying — or, in this case, watching someone dear to you die — does strange things to the mind. Makes it think along tangents.

Makes it remember things that it might have otherwise thought unimportant.

Grandpa Smedry was going to die. Bastille was going to die. Sing was going to die. And, strangely, at that very moment, I noticed the lantern that still stood on a pole at the very center of the room. The lantern holder . . . it looked something like a rutabaga.

Rutabaga, I thought. *I've heard that word recently. Rutabaga . . . fire over the inheritance!*

I scrambled forward. Blackburn spun. I threw myself toward the Lenses of Rashid — but I didn't grab them. I grabbed a Lens sitting next to them.

The Firebringer's Lens.

Blackburn's foot came down on my arm. I cried out, dropping the Lens, and a pair of Librarian soldiers quickly grabbed me. They yanked me to my feet and pulled me backward, one holding each of my arms.

Blackburn shook his head. From the corner of my eye, I

could barely make out a Librarian finally tackling Bastille. She struggled, but three others helped him hold her.

"My, my, my," Blackburn said. "And here you all are, captured again." He looked over at Grandpa Smedry, but the old man was obviously no threat. Grandpa Smedry was dazed, his leg bleeding, his face puffing up from bruises he'd apparently been putting off since his torture.

Blackburn bent down, picking up the Firebringer's Lens. "A Firebringer's Lens," he said. "You should have known better than to try and use one of these against me, boy. I'm far more powerful than you."

Blackburn turned the Lens over in his fingers. "I'm glad you brought me one, however. There weren't any in my collection — they're quite rare." Then he picked up the Lenses of Rashid. "And these. Supposedly the most powerful Lenses ever forged. Didn't your son spend his entire life gathering the sands to make these, old Smedry?"

Grandpa Smedry didn't answer.

"What a waste," Blackburn said, shaking his head. Then he raised the Firebringer's Lens to his eye. "Now, we're going to do this one more time. You are going to start answering my questions, old man. You're going to tell me the secrets of your order, and you're going to help me conquer the rest of the Free Kingdoms."

Blackburn smiled. "If you don't, I'm going to kill every one of your friends." He looked around the room. My companions stood, held by Librarian thugs. Only Bastille still struggled — Sing and Quentin looked like they had been punched a few good times in the stomach to keep them quiet.

"No," Blackburn said, "not one of the Smedrys. Your blasted Talents are too protective. Let's start with the girl." He smiled, focusing his single eye on Bastille.

"No!" Grandpa Smedry said. "Ask your questions, monster!"

"Not yet, Smedry," Blackburn said. "I have to kill one of them first, you see. Then you will understand how serious this all is."

The Firebringer's Lens began to glow.

"*NO!*" Grandpa Smedry screamed.

The Firebringer's Lens fired . . .

. . . directly *back* into Blackburn's eye.

Taking advantage of the moment, I twisted with a sudden motion, raising my hands and grabbing the arms of my captors. I sent out shocks of Talent and felt bones snap beneath my fingers. My captors cried out, jumping back and cradling broken limbs. Blackburn fell to his knees, and the Firebringer's Lens fell free, leaving a smoking socket behind. He screamed in pain.

I stepped toward the now powerless Dark Oculator. "When I grabbed the Firebringer's Lens, Blackburn, I wasn't trying to use it on you," I said. "You see, I only needed to touch it for a moment — just long enough to break it.

"It shoots *backward* now."

CHAPTER 19

I apologize for that last chapter. It was far too deep and ponderous. At this rate, it won't be long before this story departs speaking of evil Librarians, and instead turns into a terribly boring tale about a lawyer who defends unjustly accused field hands.

What do mockingbirds have to do with that, anyway?

I scooped up the Firebringer's Lens, spinning toward the thugs who still held my grandfather. The Librarians looked down at the fallen Oculator, then back up at me. I raised the Lens.

The two men dashed away. In the fury of the moment, I didn't even realize that I'd finally been able to pick up the Lens without it going off.

Grandpa Smedry slumped back against the wall in exhaustion. However, he smiled at me. "Well done, lad. Well done. You're a Smedry for certain!"

The other thugs in the room backed away, towing their hostages.

"There are two of us now," Grandpa Smedry said, righting himself, staring down the Librarians. "And your Oculator has fallen. Do you *really* want to make us mad?"

There was a moment of hesitance, and Bastille seized it. She swung up and slammed her feet into the back of the Librarian in front of her. Then she pulled herself free from her surprised captors.

The other thugs dropped Quentin and Sing, then dashed away. Bastille chased after them, cursing and kicking at one as he rushed out the door. But she let him go, grumbling quietly as she turned to make certain Sing and Quentin were all right. Both seemed well enough.

Blackburn groaned. Grandpa Smedry shook his head, looking down at the Dark Oculator.

"Should we . . . do something with him?" I asked.

"He's no threat now, lad," Grandpa Smedry said. "An Oculator without eyes is about as dangerous as a little girl."

"Excuse me?" Bastille huffed, rolling over one of the Librarian thugs that she'd knocked out before. She pulled off his sword belt and tied it around her waist.

"I apologize, dear," Grandpa Smedry said in his tired

voice. "It was just a figure of speech. Sing, would you do me a favor . . . ?"

Sing rushed over, steadying Grandpa Smedry. "Ah, very nice," Grandpa Smedry said. "Quentin, gather up any unbroken Lenses you can find. Bastille, be a dear and watch for danger at the door — there are others in this library who won't be as easily intimidated as those thugs."

"And me?" I asked.

Grandpa Smedry smiled. "You, lad, should recover your inheritance."

I turned, noticing the glasses that still lay on the ground. I walked over, picking them up. "Blackburn seemed disappointed in these."

"Blackburn was a man who focused only on one kind of power," Grandpa Smedry said. "For a man whose abilities depended on seeing, he was remarkably shortsighted."

"So . . . what do these do?" I asked.

"Try them on," Grandpa Smedry suggested.

I took off my Oculator's Lenses and put on the Rashid Lenses instead. I couldn't see any difference — no release of power, no amazing revelations.

"What am I looking for?" I asked.

"Quentin," Grandpa Smedry said, turning toward the small grad student. "What do you think?"

"I really wouldn't know," Quentin said. "The legends are all so contradictory."

I started. "Hey! I understood him!"

"That's impossible," Quentin said, still gathering Lenses off the ground. "I have my Talent on. I'm gibberish for the whole day."

"Actually, you're not," I said. "And you weren't truly gibberish those other times either. Did you know that your Talent can predict the future?"

Quentin's jaw dropped. "You can *understand* me?"

"That's what I just said. Thanks for the hint about the rutabaga, by the way."

Quentin turned toward Grandpa Smedry, who was smiling. "No, Quentin," Grandpa Smedry said. "I still can't understand you."

I stood, shocked. *What in the world . . . ?*

Then I turned, rushing over to Sing's gym bag, which lay on the side of the room. I unzipped it, digging through the ammunition to find a particular object: the book I'd swiped from the Forgotten Language room.

I opened it up to the first page. *The mechanics of forging a Truefinder's Lens is complex,* it read, *but can be understood by one who takes the proper time to study.*

I looked up, staring over at Grandpa Smedry. The old man smiled. "There are a lot of different theories about what the Sands of Rashid do, lad. Your father, however, believed in a specific theory. Translator's Lenses, they were once called — they gave the power to read, or understand, any language, tongue, or code."

I looked back at the book.

"Yes," Grandpa Smedry said tiredly. "Just wait until we show these to your father — if we can ever find him."

I spun. "So you *do* think he's alive?"

"Perhaps, lad," Grandpa Smedry said. "Perhaps. Now that we have those Lenses, perhaps we can find out for sure. I wish I'd had a way to discover sooner. If I'd known for certain whether he was dead or not, do you think I'd have let you get raised by foster parents?"

I paused. *Well, I guess the Lenses won't help me when he makes no sense.*

I opened my mouth to demand more, but Bastille cut me off. "Trouble coming! Librarian — the blond one."

I rushed over to the corridor and saw Ms. Fletcher striding toward the room, a troop of at least fifty soldiers marching behind her. These men and women were armored with shiny breastplates. A few Alivened lumbered in the background.

"Time to go, I think," I said, pushing Bastille back. Then I slammed my hand into the ground.

The floor just in front of me fell away, blocks tumbling down to the story below us. I backed away from the hole with Bastille.

"Oh, very clever, Alcatraz," Ms. Fletcher said, stopping at the pit's edge. "Now you've trapped yourself."

I smiled, raised an eyebrow, then pressed my hand against the back wall of the room. The bricks separated, mortar cracking. Sing came over and gave the wall a hefty push, toppling the bricks into the next room.

I winked at Ms. Fletcher, then reached down to slide a sword from the sheath of a fallen soldier. Ms. Fletcher stood with arms crossed, regarding Blackburn with a sour expression as I ducked out the broken wall after Sing, who was carrying Grandpa Smedry.

"Quickly, now!" Grandpa Smedry said. "We're late!"

"For what?" I asked, running beside Sing and Quentin. Bastille, of course, ran ahead of us, watching for danger.

"Why, for our dramatic exit, of course!" Grandpa Smedry said, sounding a bit tired. "Ms. Surly back there will try and cut us off at the front doors of the library."

"Well, I'll just make us another door," I said. "We'll bust out the back wall."

"Ah, lad," Grandpa Smedry said. "Haven't you realized? This entire building is inside a box of Expander's Glass — just like the gas station. Expander's Glass is *very* hard to break, even with a Talent. Besides, if you did, we'd be crushed as the entire library tried to burst out of the hole you'd made."

"Oh," I said as we reached a stairwell. "Well, then, I have another idea."

"What?" Grandpa Smedry asked.

I smiled, then reached into my pocket. I pulled out a small white rectangle: the library card we had taken off of the dungeon guard.

★

The main lobby of the library was unusually busy for a weekday evening. People milled about, perusing stacks of books, completely unaware — of course — that everything they saw was filled with Librarian fabrications.

They knew nothing of Alivened, of Librarian cults, of Smedrys, or of Lenses. They just wanted a good book to read. (None of them were, unfortunately, able to check out this volume. Not because it was banned — which it is — but because it simply hadn't been written yet. Those poor people may never know the joy they missed out on.)

Small children looked through picture books. Parents checked out the latest thrillers. The rebellious, trouble-making types looked through the fantasy section. A few unfortunate kids ended up with meaningful books about dysfunctional families.

Few of the people noticed the large number of Librarians gathering behind the front desk. Fewer still noticed that these Librarians were oddly muscular. What *nobody* noticed, however, were the weapons carefully stashed behind the counter. Ms. Fletcher stood at the front of the group. She wished to avoid making an incident — but when incidents *were* necessary, they could be contained. Smedrys were far more difficult.

Despite the buildup of Librarian troops, most of the people in the room went about their libraryish activities. All in all, there was a sense of peace about the room. It was the joy and simple contentment that comes from being around books, Librarian sanctioned or not.

That peace ended abruptly as a door at the back of the room burst open, and a group of dinosaurs rushed in.

It didn't matter that the dinosaurs carried books. It didn't matter that they were smaller than one might expect. It didn't matter that most of them wore clothing. They were dinosaurs — and they were very, *very* realistic.

The screaming started a second later.

Mothers grabbed children. Men cursed, demanding to know if this was "some kind of joke!" Librarians stood, shocked. Their hesitation cost them greatly, for within seconds there was an air of general chaos in the room.

That was when I burst through the door, carrying a sword (something I still figured I should have had all along). I was followed by Bastille Crystin, dressed in her stylish silver clothing. Quentin followed in his tuxedo, carrying Sing's gym bag, now filled with Oculator's Lenses. Sing came last, wearing his blue kimono and carrying Grandpa Smedry.

The dinosaurs dashed ahead of us, inadvertently crowding the people against the checkout counters. A few Librarian thugs broke through, but the others got trapped behind the desk, blocked by a horde of frightened people and excited dinosaurs.

Bastille met the first Librarian thug. She ducked his sword swing, then shoved him aside. He fell as she hopped over him, waving her sword toward the crowd. The people shied back in confused fear.

A Librarian behind the counter raised a crossbow.

That's new, I thought, moving between the man and Bastille. I stared down the crossbow bolt, thinking about just how dangerous it was. This last bit was, of course, to convince myself. I was beginning to get the hang of my Talent. It only worked at a distance when —

The crossbow's bowstring snapped free, flipping the crossbow bolt uselessly into the air. The Librarian watched it, dumbfounded, and I smiled, leaving Bastille to intimidate the people — and therefore keep the Librarians trapped. I rushed over to pull open the front library door.

I held it for Sing and Quentin. Bastille left next, and I paused, turning and smiling at the packed room. One of the dinosaurs — the T. Rex — finally reached the checkout desk. He slammed down his pile of books, then placed the library card on top of it.

"I'd like to check these out!" he said eagerly.

Ms. Fletcher stood, arms folded as her soldiers tried to push through the crowd. She met my eyes, and I could see from her expression that she knew she was beaten.

I raised my sword to her in a gesture of farewell. The blade immediately fell free and dropped to the ground.

I stared at it for a moment. *What? I thought I was finally figuring out how to control my Talent!*

Ms. Fletcher gave me a curious expression, as if confused by my gesture, and I sighed, flipping the broken hilt into the room. Then I stepped out onto the sidewalk. Sing (still carrying my grandfather) and Quentin ran ahead, moving toward Grandpa Smedry's little black car, which still waited where it had been parked.

Bastille still stood by the door. She met my eyes. "All right, all right," she said. "You were right about the dinosaurs. This time."

I stepped aside as some brave library patrons finally pushed past me out onto the street.

"Your dinosaur friends are just going to get caught again," Bastille said.

"Charles said he'd try to get them to leave in the confusion," I said, joining her as we ran across the street. "It's the best we can do."

And it really was. Honestly, you have no idea how hard it is to work with dinosaurs. It's no wonder the Librarians made up the myth about them going extinct — pretty much everyone in the Free Kingdoms wishes that one were true.

Sing set Grandpa Smedry in the passenger seat of the car, and Quentin squeezed into the backseat. Then Sing took the driver's seat — holding the useless steering wheel as the car took off. Bastille's silver sports car pulled up just a second later. She climbed in, but I paused. My door had no handle. Finally, Bastille opened the door by rapping on the inside dash. "The inner door handle is gone," she said, frowning.

"That's very strange," I said, sliding into the car. "Now, can we get going?"

She smiled, throwing the car into gear, then she slammed down on the pedal. I turned, watching out the back window. Behind us, a bunch of Librarians had finally managed to push their way out of the building. They watched in dismay as Bastille's car squealed away.

I smiled, turning back around. "I assume you have ways of making sure that the Librarians don't just have some of their police pick us up?"

"They don't work that way," Bastille said. "The Librarians keep as few people as possible informed about the true nature of the world. Most governments don't know that they're being manipulated. Now that we're outside of the Librarian central base, we should have a little breathing room. Especially since we neutralized their Oculator."

I nodded, resting back in my chair. "That's good to hear. I think I've had enough sneaking, chasing, and other ridiculousness for one day."

Bastille smiled, taking a sharp corner. "You know, Alcatraz, you're a bit less annoying than most Smedrys."

I smiled. "Guess I'll just have to practice some more, then."

CHAPTER 20

All right. It's true. I lied to you.

You have undoubtedly figured out that there is no altar made of outdated encyclopedias in this book. There is no harrowing situation where I lay, strapped to said altar, about to be sacrificed. There is no dagger-wielding Librarian about to slice me open and spill my blood into the void to complete a dark ritual. No sharks, no pit of acidic magma.

That's all in the sequel. You didn't really think I'd be able to tell my entire story in one book, did you?

Grandpa Smedry's car puttered along the street. It was dark out — after escaping the library, we had evacuated the gas station, then spent the night and entire next day recovering in the team's safe house (a mock hamburger stand called Sand-burgers).

"Grandfather?" I asked as we drove.

"Yes, lad?"

"What do we do now?"

Grandpa Smedry sat for a moment, turning the wheel in random directions. He looked far better after a night's rest — he had gained back enough strength to begin arriving late to his pain again, and now he was doling it out in very small amounts. He looked almost like his chipper old self.

"Well," he finally said, "there is a great deal to be done. The Free Kingdoms are losing the battle against the Librarians. Most of the outright fighting is happening in Mokia right now, though the work behind the scenes in other kingdoms is just as dangerous."

"What will happen if Mokia does fall?" I asked.

"The Librarians will fold it into their empire," Grandpa Smedry said. "It will take a decade or two before it's fully integrated — the Librarians will have to begin changing the history books across the entire world, making up a new history for the region."

I nodded. "And . . . my parents are part of this war?"

"Very big parts," Grandpa Smedry said. "They're very important people."

"So important," I asked quietly, "that they couldn't be bothered to raise me?"

Grandpa Smedry shook his head. "No, lad. That's not it at all."

"Then why?" I asked, frustrated. "What was this all about? Why leave me to the Librarians all these years?"

"It will make sense if you think about it, lad."

"I don't really want to think about it at the moment," I snapped.

Grandpa Smedry smiled. "Information, Alcatraz. It was all about information. Perhaps you've noticed, but the rest of us don't quite fit into your world."

I nodded.

"You have information, lad," Grandpa Smedry said. "Important information. You understand the lies the Librarians are teaching — and you understand their culture. That makes you important. Very important."

"So, my parents gave me up so that they could make a *spy* out of me?" I asked.

"It was a very hard decision, my boy," Grandpa Smedry said quietly. "And they did not make it lightly. But even when you were a baby, they knew you would rise to the challenge. You are a Smedry."

"And there was no other way?" I demanded.

"I know it's hard to understand, lad. And, truth be told,

I often questioned their decision. But . . . well, how many people from other countries have you known who could speak your language perfectly?"

"Not many."

"The more different a language is from your own," Grandpa Smedry said, "the more difficult it is to sound like a native. For some languages, I'm convinced it's impossible. The difference between our world and yours isn't as much a matter of language as it is a matter of understanding. I can see that I don't quite fit in here, but I can't see *why*. It's been the same for all of our operatives. We needed someone on the inside — someone who understood the way Librarians think, the way they live."

I sat quietly for a long moment. "So," I finally said, "why aren't my parents here? Why did you have to come get me?"

"I can't really answer that, Alcatraz. You know we lost track of your father some years ago, just after you were born. I kind of hoped I'd find him here, on your thirteenth birthday, come to deliver the sands himself. That obviously didn't happen."

"You have no idea where he is, then?"

Grandpa Smedry shook his head. "He is a good man —

and a good Oculator. My instincts tell me that he's alive, though I have no real proof of that. He must be about something important, but for the life of me, I can't figure out what it is!"

"And my mother?" I asked.

Grandpa Smedry didn't reply immediately. So, I turned to a slight tangent — something that had been bothering me for some time. "When I wore the Tracker's Lenses back in the library, I was able to see your footprints for a long, long time."

"That's not surprising," Grandpa Smedry said.

"And," I said, "when you came into my house, you identified my room with the Tracker's Lenses because you saw so many footprints leading into it. But I'd only walked out of there once that day. So, the other sets of footprints must have been hours — or even days — old."

"True," Grandpa Smedry said.

"So," I said, "the Tracker's Lenses work differently for family."

"Not differently, lad," Grandpa Smedry said. "Family members are part of you, and so they're part of what you know best. Their tracks tend to hang around for a long time, no matter how little you think you know them."

I sat quietly in my seat. "I saw Ms. Fletcher's footprints hours after she'd made them," I finally said.

"Not surprising."

I closed my eyes. "Why did she and my father break up?"

"He fell in love with a Librarian, lad," Grandpa Smedry said. "Marrying her wasn't the wisest decision he ever made. They thought they could make it work."

"And they were wrong?"

"Apparently," Grandpa Smedry said. "Your father saw something in her — something that I've never been able to see. She isn't exactly the most loyal of Librarians, and your father thought that would make her more lenient to our side. But . . . I think she's only interested in herself. She married your father for his Talent, I'm convinced. Either way, I think that she was another reason that your father agreed to let you be raised in Librarian lands. That way, your mother could see you. He still loved her, I'm afraid. Probably still does, poor fool."

I closed my eyes. *She sold the Sands of Rashid to Blackburn. My father's life's work, my inheritance. And . . . Blackburn implied that she would sell me too.* I didn't know how to think about what I felt. For some reason, all the danger — all the threats — I'd been through during the last few days hadn't felt as disturbing to me as the knowledge that my mother lived.

And that she was on the wrong side.

Grandpa Smedry's car puttered to a stop. I opened my eyes, looking out the window with a frown. I recognized the street we were on. Joan and Roy Sheldon — my latest foster family, the one whose kitchen I had burned — lived just a few houses down.

"Why are we here?" I asked.

"You remember when I first gave you your Oculator's Lenses, lad?"

"Sure."

"I asked you a question then," Grandpa Smedry said. "I asked why you had burned down your family's kitchen. You didn't answer."

"I thought about it, though," I said. "I'm figuring things out. I'm getting better with my Talent."

"Alcatraz, lad," Grandpa Smedry said, laying a hand on my shoulder. "That question wasn't just about your Talent. You keep asking about your parents, keep wondering why they were so willing to abandon you. Well, did you ever think to wonder why *you* abandoned so many families?"

"I have thought about it," I said. "Or, at least, I have

recently. And perhaps I was a little hard on them. But it wasn't *only* my fault. They couldn't handle it when I broke things."

"Maybe some of them," Grandpa Smedry said. "But how many of them did you really give a chance?"

I knew he was right, of course. And yet, knowing something is very different from feeling it. And at that moment, I was feeling all the same emotions I felt every time parents gave me away.

I felt a twist in my gut. It was happening again, and this time it wasn't my fault. I'd tried. I'd tried not to push Grandpa Smedry away. And now it was happening anyway.

"You're trying to get rid of me," I whispered.

Grandpa Smedry shook his head. "Information, lad! It's all about *information*. You thought those families were going to give you up, so you acted first. You *made* them get rid of you. But you had bad information.

"I'm not trying to abandon you. We have a lot of work to do, you and I. However, you need to go back and spend some time with those who have loved you. You need to make your peace with them if you're ever going to understand yourself well enough to help us win this war."

"Blackburn didn't think information was all that important," I snapped.

"And how'd he end up?" Grandpa Smedry said, smiling.

"But he beat you," I said. "In the Oculators' Duel. He was stronger."

"Yes, he was," Grandpa Smedry said. "He worked very hard to be able to beat a person like me in a contest like that. He put out his eye so that he would be stronger with offensive Lenses, and he collected other Lenses that would let him fight effectively.

"But, in doing so, he gave up the ability to see as well. Alcatraz, everything we do is about seeing! If he'd *seen* just a little better, he would have noticed your trick. If he'd *seen* a little better, he'd have realized that by putting out his eye and focusing on the powers that let him win battles, he handicapped himself in larger, far more important ways. Perhaps if he'd *seen* a little more, he'd have realized that those Translator's Lenses you have are far more powerful than any Firebringer's Lens."

I sat back, trying to sort out my thoughts — and my emotions. It was hard to focus on any one feeling — regret, anxiety, anger, confusion. I still couldn't believe that

Grandpa wanted me to stay with Joan and Roy. I glanced at the house. "Hey, there's no hole in the side of it!"

"The Librarians would have fixed that before your foster parents got home," Grandpa Smedry said. "They try to keep things quiet, work on the underground — something like that hole would have attracted too much attention to this house, and therefore to you."

"Won't it be dangerous for me to be here?" I asked.

"Probably," Grandpa Smedry said. "But it will be dangerous for *you* everywhere. And, we have some . . . means of keeping you safe here, for a little while at least."

I nodded slowly.

"They'll be happy to see you, lad," Grandpa Smedry said.

"I don't know about that," I said. "I burned down their kitchen."

"Try them."

I shook my head. "I still can't control it, Grandfather," I said quietly. "My Talent. I thought I was getting the hang of it, but I still break things all the time — things I don't want to."

Grandpa Smedry smiled. "Perhaps. But when it counted, you broke that Firebringer's Lens in *exactly* the right way.

You didn't just shatter it or make it stop working. You made it work wrong, but made it work right for you. That shows real promise, lad."

I looked over at the Sheldons' house again. "You'll . . . come for me, won't you?"

"Of course I will, lad!"

I took a deep breath. "All right, then. Do you want to take the Translator's Lenses with you?"

"They're your inheritance, lad. It wouldn't be right. You keep them."

I nodded. Grandpa Smedry smiled, then reached over to give me a hug. I held on tight — tighter than I'd probably intended.

Grandfather, cousins, perhaps even my father, I thought. *I have family.*

Finally, I let go, then got out of the car. I looked up at the house again. *I've always had family,* I thought. *Not always the Sheldons, but someone. People willing to give me a home. I guess it's about time I admitted that.*

I closed the door, then looked in through the window.

"Don't break anything!" Grandpa Smedry said.

"Just come for me," I said. "Don't be late."

"Me?" Grandpa Smedry asked. "Late?"

Then he rapped on the dash of the car, and it began to hum. I watched it pull away, watched it until it was gone. Then I walked up the street to the house. I paused on the doorstep.

I could still faintly smell smoke.

I knocked on the door. Roy opened it. He stood, stupefied, for a moment. Then he yelled in surprise, grabbing me in a hug. "Joan!" he cried.

She rushed around the corner. "Alcatraz?"

Roy handed me over to her. She grabbed me in a tight embrace.

"When the caseworker called," Roy said, "asking where you'd gone . . . well, we assumed you'd run off for good, kiddo."

"You didn't get into trouble, did you?" Joan asked, looking at me sternly.

I shrugged. "I don't know. I knocked down two floors, one wall, and a few doors, I think. Nothing too bad."

Joan and Roy shared a look, then smiled, and took me in.

Hours later, after giving them some reasonable lies about where I'd been, after having a good meal, and after accepting their pleas that I stay with them for at least a little while longer, I walked up to my room.

I sat down on my bed, trying to think through the things that had happened to me. Oddly, I didn't find the Librarians, the Alivened, or the Lenses to be the most strange of the recent events. The strangest things to me were the changes I saw in myself.

I *cared*. And it had all happened because of a simple package in the mail. . . .

My head snapped up. There, sitting on my desk, was the empty box, beside its brown wrapper. I stood and walked across the room. I flattened out the packaging, noting the stamp that I'd investigated, the address written in faded ink . . . and the scribbles up the side of the paper. The ones I'd assumed had come from someone trying to get the ink in his pen to flow.

With trembling hands, I reached into my pocket and pulled out the Translator's Lenses — the Lenses of Rashid. I slipped them on. The scribble immediately changed into legible words.

Son,

Congratulations! If you can read this, then you have managed to craft Lenses of Rashid from the sands I sent you. I knew you'd be able to do it!

I must tell you that I am afraid. I fear that I've stumbled on something powerful — something more important, and more dangerous, than any of us expected. The Lenses of Rashid were only the beginning! The Forgotten Language leads to clues, stories, legends about the Smedry Talents and —

Well, I can't say more here. By the time you get this package, much time will have passed. Thirteen years. Perhaps I'll have solved the problem by then, but I suspect not. The Lenses that let me see where you will be living at age thirteen have also given me a warning that my task will not be done by then. But I can only see vaguely into the future — the Oracle's Lenses are far from perfect! What I see makes me even more worried.

Once I have confirmation that this box reached you without being intercepted, I will send you further information. I have the other set of Rashid Lenses — with them, I can write in the Forgotten Language, and only you will be able to read my messages.

304

For now, simply know that I'm proud of you, and that I love you.

Your father,

Attica Smedry

I put the paper down, stunned. It was at that moment that I heard a rapping on my window. Instead of a raven outside, however, I saw the mustached face of Grandpa Smedry.

I frowned, walking over and opening the window. Grandpa Smedry stood on a ladder that appeared to have extended from the back of his little black automobile.

"Grandpa?" I asked. "What are you doing here?"

"What?" he asked. "I came for you, as promised."

"As promised?" I asked. "But you only left me a few hours ago."

"Yes, yes," Grandpa Smedry said. "I know, I'm late. Come on, lad! We've got work to do. Are you packed yet?"

Grandpa Smedry began to climb back down the ladder.

"Wait," I said, sticking my head out the window. "Packed? I thought I was staying here with Joan and Roy!"

"What?" Grandpa Smedry said, looking back up. "Edible Eddings, boy! This city is crawling with Librarians. It was dangerous enough to give you a chance to come back and say good-bye!"

"But you said I had to spend some time with them!"

"A few hours, lad," Grandpa Smedry said, "to apologize for the trouble you'd given them. What did you expect? That I'd leave you here all summer, in the exact place where your enemies know where to look? With people that aren't even your family? In a place you don't really like, and that is depressingly normal compared to the world you've grown to love? Doesn't that sound a little stupid and contrived to you?"

I raised a relieved hand to my head. "Yeah," I noted, "now that you mention it, who *would* do something silly like that? Let me go get my things and write a note to Joan and Roy. Oh, and you have to see what's written on this package!"

I rushed back into the room, pulling out a gym bag to begin packing. Outside, I heard Grandpa Smedry's car hum quietly to life.

I smiled. Everything felt right. Weird, true, but *right*.

It was about time.

EPILOGUE

So, that's how it began. Not as spectacular as some have claimed, I know, but it felt incredible enough to me at the time.

Now, I'll be the first to admit that those first couple of days had a profound effect on me, shaking me slightly out of the self-indulgent rebelliousness that I had fallen into. The thing is, if I could go back, I'd still tell myself not to go with Grandpa Smedry on that strange, unfortunate day.

The things I learned during that first infiltration — trust, self-confidence, bravery — might seem good at first glance. However, the changes I experienced were just setting me up for my eventual fall. You'll see what I mean.

For now I hope this narrative was enough to show that even supposed heroes have flaws. Let this be your warning — I'm not the person that you think I am. You'll see.

With regret,

Alcatraz Smedry

And so, untold millions screamed out in pain, and then were suddenly silenced. I hope you're happy.

(This was included for anyone who skipped forward to read the last page of the book. For the rest of you — the ones who reached the last page in the proper, honorable, and Smedry-approved manner — those untold millions are cheering in praise of your honesty.

They'll probably throw you a party.)

ABOUT THE AUTHOR

"Brandon Sanderson" is the pen name of Alcatraz Smedry. His Hushlander editor forced him to use a pseudonym, since these memoirs are being published as fiction.

Alcatraz actually knows a person named Brandon Sanderson. That man, however, is a fantasy writer, and is therefore prone to useless bouts of delusion in literary form. Alcatraz has it on good authority that Brandon Sanderson is actually illiterate and dictates his thick, overly long fantasy tomes to his potted plant, Count Duku.

It is widely assumed that Brandon went mad several years ago, but few people can tell because his writing is so strange anyway. He spends his time going to science fiction movies, eating popcorn and goat cheese (separately), and trying to warn people about the dangers of the Great Kitten Conspiracy.

He's had his library card revoked on seventeen different occasions.

ACKNOWLEDGMENTS

Thanks to my agents, Joshua Bilmes (who single-handedly transformed this manuscript from being a whimsical idea into a full-blown super-project) and Steve Mancino, who exceeded my expectations wildly in finding the book a home.

And, speaking of that home, Anica Rissi — my editor at Scholastic — took fantastic care of this book, helping make it the best book possible. Her tireless work is well appreciated, and the same goes for all of the wonderful people over at Scholastic.

As for alpha readers, I'd like to thank Stacy Whitman, Heather Kirby, Kristina Kugler, Peter and Karen Ahlstrom, Kaylynn ZoBell, Isaac Thegn Skarstedt, Ethan Skarstedt, Leif Ethan Skarstedt, Benjamin R. Olsen, Matisse Hales, Lauren Sanderson, Alan Layton, Janette Layton, Nathan Hatfield, Krista Olsen, C. Lee Player, Eric J. Ehlers, and

Emily Sanderson. Special thanks to my grandmother, Beth Sanderson, for suggesting this project.

Also, I'd like to give a special acknowledgment to Janci Patterson who worked tirelessly to slay the typo demons in this manuscript. (Not that I didn't manage to sneak a few more in afterward.)

Finally, a thanks to all of the evil librarians out there. It's partially their fault that I ended up being a writer instead of something useful, like a plumber or a foghorn repair technician. It's poetic justice that I would now use my nefarious talent to expose you all for what you really are.

Brandon Sanderson